Also from Dagger Books
by JJ Dare

False Positive

Visit JJ Dare at www.jacketblind.com

FALSE WORLD

By

JJ Dare

Dagger Books
Published by Second Wind Publishing, LLC.
Kernersville

Dagger Books
Second Wind Publishing, LLC
931-B South Main Street, Box 145
Kernersville, NC 27284

This book is a work of fiction. Names, characters, locations and events are either a product of the author's imagination, fictitious or use fictitiously. Any resemblance to any event, locale or person, living or dead, is purely coincidental.

Copyright © 2009 by JJ Dare

All rights reserved, including the right of reproduction in whole or part in any format.

First Dagger Books edition published August, 2009.
Dagger Books, Running Angel, and all production design are trademarks of Second Wind Publishing, used under license.

For information regarding bulk purchases of this book, digital purchase and special discounts, please contact the publisher at www.secondwindpublishing.com

Cover design by Stacy Castanedo

Manufactured in the United States of America

ISBN 978-1-935171-38-6

Thanks to:

Rene' for reading,
Rachel and Robyn for supporting,
Dan for encouraging,
and Donald and Kaytie just because.

—JJ Dare

1.

There was nothing normal about the town of Normal.

In the middle of a lush green state, the barren town was nothing if not abnormal. There were no trees, no grass, nothing much but barren, dry land. It was as if a bomb had been dropped in the area and the blast had sucked the life out of everything.

The air was stagnant. Wind did not blow, and there was no such thing as a cool evening breeze. The temperature ranged from hot to hotter. Seasons were a joke: winter and fall lasted about two weeks and for the rest of the year, blistering heat ruled.

The rural area surrounding the town was fertile with crops of corn and beans and other imaginable or unimaginable vegetables and fruits. The corporately owned farms around Normal were abundant with life of all sorts.

Normal was different. It was as if the town had been cursed with a vast, dry blight that no amount of water could help. The few weeds that dared to grow quickly died under the oppressive arid heat.

A long time ago, something had happened to kill the ground around Normal. Some said it was nuclear testing. Others thought it was ground contamination from a power plant a few miles away. Still others swore it was barren from alien spacecraft which had landed and scorched the land.

Buildings around the town appeared dry and brittle and looked as if they might topple down with the slightest gust of wind. However, that was not a problem since no wind blew in Normal.

The air was so hot, sweat dried on the skin as soon as it formed. Lip balm and lotion were mainstays of men, women, and children alike. Cracked skin was a common ailment the local clinic treated on a regular basis.

Life was strange in Normal. Everyone moved at a much slower pace than normal. All the people in the town knew each other and, more often than not, spent most of the day trying to keep cool and the rest of the time complaining about the heat. Aside from the continuous topic of heat, the mainstay of the town was gossip.

The new building built at the edge of town was a strange bird. It had numerous driveways, but few windows. The top was covered with satellite dishes. There was a guard house at the entrance and a steel gate enclosed the structure and the barbed wire fence surrounding the two hundred acres behind the building.

A separate water supply station and powerhouse stood at the back. Three other smaller buildings stood apart from the others, but their purpose was unknown.

The crews who built the structure were not local. They were all clean-cut and muscular, all wearing the same type of dark brown t-shirts and work pants, and all sporting dark, wrap-around sunglasses. At a distance, you could not tell one of them from the other.

The townspeople of Normal were having a field day speculating about the owner of the building's business, mainly, what kind of business needed such security and secrecy. From front porches to lawn chairs, the highlight of the past month had been binocular-watching the comings and goings of the work crews at all hours of the day and night.

It did not matter, though. As far as anyone could tell, there was no one person in charge and there was no one person not in charge. No one from the structure ever came into town. The land was owned by a corporation, and when the local historian had tried to find out the names of the executives of the company, he had come up almost empty.

The corporation was a privately held company with one board member by the name of John Q. Smith. There was no other information on Smith, no address, no phone number, nothing.

Taxes were paid on time and the bills were sent to a post office box in New York City. Since the structure was just outside of city limits, there were no papers filed with the town that might have contained more information about the mysterious owner.

Something else strange was happening in Normal. One by one, the population of fifty-five was dwindling down. Calvert Mitchum was the first to go with the excuse that he was moving to Albinville to be closer to his mother.

His mother had died over thirty years before.

Jeff Rankin and his family were next. One day they were going about their business and the next day they were packing up all of their belongings. When a neighbor asked, Jeff told her that he had gotten a transfer and had to leave immediately.

The neighbor did not buy it, especially considering the looks of fear and excitement on the faces of Jeff and his family. Something had happened and it had scared the crap out of them and, at the same time, had made them all exhilarated to the point of silliness.

One by one, people disappeared. The local historian was the last to go and he was prepared to fight until he came face to face with the emotionless men who offered him the deal of a lifetime.

For a sinfully wonderful amount of money, the historian sold his house and soul to the devil. The only catch was he could never, ever talk about where he had come from nor who he had dealt with nor what they had given to him.

To reinforce this, the emotionless men who had made him the deal showed him a photo album of people who had broken their end of the bargain.

The historian vomited into the garbage can after looking at the pictures.

Just to get the point across, again, – and they really did not need to because he got it the first time – the nameless men made him watch a video on the LCD display of a camcorder they had brought in.

The historian vomited once more.

They never told him he had a choice, but he felt that he could either take their offer or end up in the photo album or captured on video on the camcorder. He was given one minute to decide.

With money in his pocket and an aching arm from a strange hypodermic shot they told him was part of the bargain, the historian left town that very day. The nameless men told him before he left that they had injected a small tracer in his arm and if he tried to remove it, it would implode in his vein and cause a massive stroke.

In addition, the tracer would pinpoint his location at all times and would also monitor everything he said and did. If he broke the pact he had made with the faceless men, he would be found immediately and would become the poster boy for pain and mutilation.

He did not even look back as he left the town.

With the last person gone, Normal briefly became a ghost town, but that soon changed. The corporation came in and deconstructed the entire place. New buildings went up almost overnight and a company store with everything under the sun was up and running within a week.

They even went so far as to reroute the roads leading into town. To get into the town at this point, one would have to go through military-type checkpoints. Outsiders were always turned away.

Although the entire town was not fenced, that did not mean anything. The latest in security parameters surrounded the town and nothing got in or out without injury or death. The first casualty was a vagrant traveling cross-country hoping to score some cash from the people of Normal.

When he unknowingly stepped over the parameter after blatantly ignoring the no-trespassing-violators-will-be-shot-dead signs, the tingling he felt starting at his feet quickly raced to the top of his head. Vibrating violently, his teeth cracked as he uncontrollably snapped his mouth open and shut as hard as possible.

Paralyzed into position, he could not move a muscle or even blink. Smoke spiraled off the vagrant's fingertips as a current continued to race through his body. He felt nothing; his pain sensors had short-circuited.

After a preset time, the current automatically turned off.

The vagrant fell to the ground, clawing at the dirt as his body twitched and convulsed its way to death. His mind had gone and his body was reacting on a primal level.

The clean-up crew standing around him as he died waited for the all clear before loading him onto the back of what they called the "morbid" truck for the short ride to the crematorium.

They never found dead animals around the parameter security fence. Unfortunately, that just went to show that even though animals could not read the signs, they were smarter than some people who did read the warnings, but chose to ignore them with fatal consequences.

The new Normal was on the map but not on the map. Airspace over and around the town had been restricted on highest orders. The rerouted road kept the bulk of the traffic away from Normal, and the occasional lost traveler was quickly and politely escorted back to the main highway.

Instead of a dry, dusty, barren place, Normal was soon transformed into a lush, fertile area that blended with the lush, fertile areas surrounding the town. This was due in part to the emergence of underground springs the original townspeople thought had dried up, but, with the right tools were quickly opened up.

Green replaced dusty brown as the new color in Normal. Large trees were imported and planted, bushes thrived, grass grew, and flowers bloomed. Had the original townspeople been there to witness it, they would have been amazed at the transformation. Even more so, they would have been amazed at the occasional breeze that was caught in the trees and directed toward the town.

Although there were few people roaming the streets at any given time, the town was not silent. There was a busy hum of activity at all hours. Regardless of the time, there were always people coming and going. The sun and moon meant nothing to the new residents of Normal.

That is, the sun and moon meant nothing save for one.

2.

Joe Daniels was confused. And his head hurt like a mother. His vision was blurry and he felt wobbly. He was thirsty, but when he tried to lick his lips, his swollen tongue would not move.

Terrified, Joe's first thought was he was paralyzed from his mouth down. As his fuzzy brain cleared, he realized he could not move his tongue because he was wearing a mouth guard.

Still fuzzy and confused, Joe wondered who had tackled him hard enough to knock him out and why could not he hear the roar of the crowds on the football field. As his brain gradually cleared, he thought he must have been knocked hard enough to burst his eardrums.

Slowly, his senses were returning and with them, the pain. His nose felt like a thousand shards of glass were moving around and around inside. His head was throbbing with each heartbeat. His left arm felt as though it had been caught in a vise and twisted until the bones snapped.

The good news was his hearing was fine. He could hear, but could not see the people who were constantly attending to him. He heard the rustle of their clothes as they moved quietly in the room and occasionally, he would hear their soft voices as they spoke amongst themselves.

He could not move. He was so constricted the only thing mobile were his eyes. As the hours passed, he rode a roller coaster of pain when he was awake and a hard sleep when the woman with the surgical mask gave him a wonderful injection of knock-out drugs.

When he was awake, his eyes followed the paths of the sun and moon as they slowly crossed the sky above his head. Because of the way he was positioned in the bed and because of the vise grip on his head, the glass ceiling above him was the only direction he could look.

As he continued his return to coherency, he would see his caretakers, but only when they were directly above him.

It did not matter, though, because these people were only eyes to him behind the surgical masks they always wore.

He was much more interested in the sun and the moon.

He was not sure how long he had been in the half-fugue state, but somewhere around what he thought was his fourth day of internment, his mind began to clear. As the pain in his head started to subside, his memories returned.

And they returned with a wallop.

As the memories flooded back, there were times when he welcomed his happy shot of knock-out drugs. He remembered the brutality of what he had been through and the darkness of what was to come.

His first coherent thought was of his Beanie. Her life and her death. The message from Todd right before Joe's deadly confrontation with the Presatical. "She's not dead," it had read. He had been sitting at a table in the coffee shop in Avvel across the street from the restaurant where he was meeting and, hopefully, killing the man responsible for her death. He had knowingly and purposely been on a suicide mission.

When he got the message, everything changed. He could not take a chance on dying if Beanie was still alive. If what the message said was true, he had to get to her and protect her. It was not that the Presatical's death would be abandoned; rather, it would have to be delayed.

Beanie was his first and only mission right then.

He had shuddered to think what might have happened if he had not received Todd's message in time. Whether or not Joe succeeded in his attempt to assassinate the Presatical, the hated man's bodyguards would have surely killed Joe.

As he packed up his laptop, he had seen the group of black cars pull up to the restaurant. As a man emerged surrounded by bodyguards, Joe knew that it was not the Presatical. He did not know who this smallish man with thinning brown hair was, but he did know he was a decoy.

Walking on the opposite side of the road, Joe glanced in the opened door of the second car and saw a polished shoe glistening in the dark recesses of the back seat. So, he had come after all; however, he was not going into the restaurant to be a sitting duck. Instead, he would have been a sitting duck inside his car.

What an idiot, Joe thought. Although the Presatical could not know that Joe already knew what he really looked like, it was still a stupid move on the Presatical's part. Sheepishly, Joe that about his own stupidity, because why in the world did he think that someone as guarded, mysterious, and private as this Presatical thing would even come out to meet Joe?

It was just a case of the stupids all around.

Joe had walked past the cars and then past a group of excited tourists who were snapping pictures of everything from the rocks in the road to the mountains in the distance to everyone walking by. Joe knew he was in a few of those pictures. He even smiled for one shot. Up until a few minutes ago, he would have shunned the digital camera, but now he did not care. He was on his way to Beanie and if his picture ended up splashed all over the Internet, so be it. He had much more important things to do.

As he walked to the edge of town toward the bus stop, he noticed a young girl following him. He had first become aware of her when the hairs on the back his neck had stood up – a sure sign someone was watching him.

Every time he stopped, she stopped. When he hurried along, she picked up her pace. He doubled back across the street and so did she. He could not believe how obvious she was and because his attention was focused on her, he did not see the see the man step in front of him and swing at his face with a billy club.

Stunned with a blinding pain to his nose, Joe went down to his knees. As the man picked up and pushed him toward the edge of a steep gully behind a row of stores on the main street of Avvel, Joe could not protect himself because of the pain. Stumbling blindly, Joe tripped and fell down on the ground at the top of the gully.

The second to last thing Joe remembered before waking up days or weeks or months latter to the pain and the sun and the moon, was the hourglass pupils of the man as he bent down to check Joe's breathing and deliver what Joe believed to be the coup de grace to the top of his head.

The last thing on his mind before he lost consciousness as he tumbled down toward the rocks at the bottom of the steep ditch was of Beanie and of his failure, once again, to protect her.

He remembered all of this and more days or weeks or months later as he watched the sun, then the moon.

He was somewhere being cared for by a group of people he did not know. Joe struggled to get a timeframe in his head, but it was useless without some kind of reference. He had no idea how long he had been in a semi-conscious state.

On the day his memory returned, he was allowed to sit up with help. The nurse-like person who helped him was gentle, but totally uncommunicative. Joe could not say a word, because, once he sat up he realized that, in addition to the mouth guard, his jaw was held rigidly in place by a hard, plastic contraption.

Gingerly feeling the rest of his body as he cautiously sat up, he was aware of three things besides the trapped jaw: his left arm was in a lightweight cast, his nose was taped across the bridge with some type of rigid medical tape, and his head was wrapped with a large, stretchy bandage.

His chest felt tight. As he felt around with his right hand, he discovered his ribs were wrapped tightly with wide bandages. Of course he had broken ribs because what was a fall down a steep gully without broken ribs?

His body was wounded, but his mind was returning. He remembered every single thing that had happened to him from the beginning of the whole, horrid ordeal to the tumble into the ravine.

He remembered when the keys were destroyed. Their ending had been his beginning, only he hadn't known it at the time. He was the only one who held all of the keys in his mind. His photographic memory knew each and every one of them. Without the keys, the ringleader of the world, the one they called the Presatical, was powerless to restore order and balance.

The Book of the Deceived was not a book at all. It was passed down to generation after generation of special idiot savants, and it was their memories that held the checks and balances for the world. Warfare throughout the centuries was not determined by the strongest; it was negotiated and bought, and the Presatical was the broker of the sordid deals.

The Book held the records of all the wars fought for centuries. Nation fought nation, but the outcome had already been determined before the first sword was raised or the first gun was fired. So as not to lose everything, nations within the Presatical's care knowingly sacrificed men while others lost land. To them, the loss of men was much less of a loss than that of land.

Meetings between opposing world leaders took place all of the time. Those who accepted the Presatical's decisions lost very little. Those nations who did not abide by the Book were annihilated, disassembled, and divided among the other nations. Their leaders were punished with death.

Like a secret United Nations, this group of leaders kept their power and their land by dealing with the devil. Human life was not sacred; it was simply numbers on the Presatical's scorecard.

All of this Joe remembered and, looking back, he realized he had been a fool to think that he, a simple man, could have toppled this evil assembly of powerful men.

Joe remembered the accident that had caused him the greatest loss of his life. He remembered Beanie in the hospital and the misery he had felt tempered by the hope when she seemed to be recovering.

He remembered bringing his wife home to convalesce and the strangeness he felt around her. He remembered discovering the woman he thought was the love of his life was more than a stranger; she was an imposter. He remembered the fateful night he was arrested for brutally killing her.

Everything came back to him: Todd's warning about the sophisticated ghoul tracking devices in his house and car, the old Indian Henry's tales of conspiracies that Joe discovered were truer than just the fanciful wanderings of an old man, and his close encounters with the unknown people who seemed to want him dead.

Joe thought of when he was tracking the man he believed responsible for everything happening to him. He had not forgotten one single detail.

As he was accustoming himself to sitting upright, he heard the door to his room open and familiar, soft voice speak:

"I heard you were awake and it looks like you are more coherent today," the voice continued as it drew closer.

Joe knew that voice. Turning slowly around, Joe faced the cold-eyed man who had rescued him once before. Although he had told Joe he would not get another chance, it looked like this man had saved him again.

"You have been out for five days. You suffered a moderate concussion, broken bridge, broken jaw, broken ribs. Your left arm is not broken, but the muscles were twisted during the fall."

The cold-eyed man watched as the emotions played across Joe's unguarded face. As he stared at Joe, he wondered, for the hundredth time, if the blow to Joe's head had rendered him useless to everyone. If he had lost the knowledge of the keys, there was no point in protecting him.

Time would tell.

"You were attacked by a radical group determined to bring the apocalypse sooner rather than later. The man who attacked you has been dealt with, as has the girl who was a collaborator. Neither will be able to harm you."

Joe listened as intently as he could, but he could feel his eyes growing heavy. Damn it, he did not want to fall asleep without finding out more, but he was helpless against the fatigue. His injured brain was overloaded.

"When you become better, we will talk again," the cold-eyed man said as he got up to leave the room.

"One more thing," he said as he turned around to face Joe before opening the door. "Do not think of leaving this room without an escort. We are in a guarded town and our security is deadly force."

As the door quietly shut, Joe felt his body relax back onto the bed as he fell asleep before his head touched the pillow.

He dreamed of the moon.

3.

Across the ocean, a man sat on a balcony overlooking a pristine garden. A full moon illuminated every plant and tree within the landscaped field. It was beautiful and tranquil, but the man paid little attention to the moonlit scene.

Again, he had had his quarry within reach. Again, his prey had slipped through his grasp, but this time it had been by the interference of two separate groups. One he was very familiar with, the Muveed Ursus; the other, not so familiar. Regardless, he had been thwarted, again, in his efforts to capture Joe Daniels.

He watched indifferently as the light from the moon played across the flowers. His mind was on his most immediate problem: the leaders of the world he held power over were closing in on him. Unless he found a way to placate them until he could open the minds of his savants, he would be crucified.

He knew it was useless to try to find a backdoor into the swirling bedlam of his charges' minds. They had been surgically altered to prevent that from happening. A rerouting of certain areas within the cortex of their brain stem had resulted in an impenetrable mind that could only be opened with a certain set of words and numbers.

Those words and numbers had been locked and guarded to prevent anyone, save the Presatical, from taking them and using them against others. The knowledge locked inside the minds of the savants was beyond priceless and contained the history of the world, the checks and balances of nations, the calculated deals for wins and losses, and the names of every world leader participating in this sordid business.

The keys had been in what should have been the safest place in the world. Should have been, but obviously was not, since a down on his luck junkie had been able to penetrate that locked and guarded place and had stolen the keys. Once he realized they were useless, he had discarded them like trash.

Joe Daniels and his combat unit had stumbled upon them, but, thinking they were trash, too, they had thrown them in a fire. The last hope of a balanced world had gone up in flames.

In a way, the Presatical had been lucky that it was Joe who had seen the keys before they were destroyed. Even though he had never interrogated him, the Presatical knew from the background he had collected on Joe, that this former commando had a memory like few others. He could recall anything he had seen, down to the finest detail.

Yes, the Presatical had been lucky. As it was, Joe was the only person who could stop the mounting chaos and bring order back to the world. He was the only one who could remember with clarity, the keys. He had, in fact, become the keys.

The others from Joe's unit had not remembered much of anything, no even with a little "gentle" persuasion. After this persuasion, their minds had turned to mush and the Presatical had told his minions to take them away. He did not know what they had done with them or where they might have taken them; he did not care, as long he was not directly involved.

That's the way it had to be. He could never be directly involved in anything. The way he kept the balance was a sterile rendering and crunching of numbers on the virtual paper locked inside his savants' minds. His hands were never dirtied.

Without the keys, his savants were not responsive and no amount of surgical probing could unlock their minds. The surgeon who had originally enhanced their minds had been under instruction to make sure it could not be reversed or altered.

He had done an excellent job.

In times past, the savants had been selected based on their specific talents. Most were rejected, but the ones chosen would be trained to remember. This instruction, in the olden times, was often brutal and many savants died as a result of "training."

Modern medicine brought a kinder, gentler invasion of the savant mind. Although research into the connection between savantism and the mind had not uncovered much, some researchers, through private funding, were more successful.

What they discovered was a new area within the prefrontal cortex that could be manipulated. The researchers named this area the anterior frontal lobe, or aft for short. Through many trials and errors, the researchers found that if the auditory and visual cortexes were flooded with a specific chemical, the aft lobe would activate and the amount of memory that could be stored there was greater than what could be downloaded into a hundred computers.

However, the downside to this manipulation was that other areas, specifically the auditory, visual, sensory, and somatosensory lobes, shrank, leaving the subject only a few steps above a vegetative state. In this state, the savant could not take care of himself and had to be monitored twenty-four hours a day.

Another effect of this treatment was the occasional flash of rebellious intelligence. One subject became so belligerent that he had to be "released" from duty. He had faked his usual stupor until his handlers left his room and then had escaped the chalet. Fortunately, he did not get very far before his handlers found him and brought him back to the chalet. The two hikers he ran into and communicated with were less fortunate.

After more trials on this particular subject, the researchers found the relationship between the induced chemical and the subject's overactive pituitary gland had given him a superior awareness. From that point forward, the pituitary gland was monitored frequently.

Most of the successful savants were very malleable. They understood the basic commands of eat, drink, and sleep. The more complex memories and commands were hardwired into their aft lobe and locked in until released by the keys.

The miracle of modern medicine made it possible to

quickly lock the memories under a key set of numbers, words, and/or phrases by way of chemical and surgical inducement. The pioneer of this radical brain manipulation was Dr. Makia Li.

Dr. Li had been a valuable asset to the Presatical for many years. His sudden death two years previously had been a huge blow. The bigger blow, however, was the reluctance of Dr. Li's protégée to take over the reins of monitoring the current savants and surgically enhancing the prospects.

Briberies, enticements, or threats had not had any effect on the man who should have taken over from Dr. Li. The Presatical had gone so far as to "invite" the man's family to the chalet for an extended stay – it did not make a difference. Dr. Li's protégée read the note left for him by the Presatical's goons that outlined what would happen to his wife and sons unless he cooperated.

As soon as Dr. Thomas Miko read that fateful note, he had turned out the lights, locked the doors, and disappeared into the night. Leaving the small seaside village of Tikati on the eastern coast of Nippon, he knew he would never return to that part of the world. His family was already lost to him: the moment they had been abducted, they were dead.

Dr. Miko ran and ran and ran, and did not stop running until he was across the world in another country. When he landed at the port city, the first thing he did was find other people from his homeland. Once he was in their part of the city, he paid to become someone else.

The Presatical's men lost Dr. Miko's trail after he arrived in the United States. All the Presatical could do now was hope that somehow, somewhere Miko would resurface. When he did, the Presatical would give him no choice.

So, for the time being, everything was up in the air. Nothing could be done to the savants to make them give up the secrets that had been so ruthlessly implanted into their minds. The only hope would be if either the doctor or Joe Daniels were captured and then convinced, one way or another, to help.

The Presatical sat in the moonlight pondering his next

move. He had come so far and accomplished so much. He had kept the world from destroying itself from senseless world-engulfing wars. He was the world's savior.

He was not going to let everything he had done end like this. He refused.

Angrily, he thought of the many times his men had been so close to that unbelievably lucky man. Each time, Joe Daniels had slipped through their grasp. Each time, he had gotten a little closer to the truth.

To make matters much worse, the Muveed Ursus had seen fit to become involved. The Presatical had tangled with this radical group more than once, and he had never come out on top. He never called these inopportune run-ins with the Ursus losses because he simply could not fathom losing. Rather, it was a draw.

Joe Daniels' trail had grown colder than ice. His last known position had been within a stone's throw of the chalet. He had been in the village that belonged to the Presatical. The Presatical's computer experts had digitally confirmed his whereabouts.

Then, he had disappeared.

Nothing had been heard from him or from his computer. There had been no further contact and nothing had shown up on message boards or blogs. No one with Joe Daniels' description had been reported either here or in the States.

Just as he had vanished for that long month after his wife's death and at the beginning of this horribly botched operation, he was missing once again. It had already been almost two weeks from the last contact Joe Daniels had made, practically in the Presatical's front yard.

As he sat in the beautiful silence, his second approached and quietly took a seat across from the Presatical.

"The committee is calling a meeting in three days," the second said. "They want you to tell them why you have not been keeping the balance."

The Presatical did not respond. He knew his second was only repeating what had been told to him by the committee. He felt no empathy for those leaders who could not control their own countries.

"There is something else," the second continued. "The committee is going to ask to have access to the savants. They are being led to believe that you no longer have the power to open the Book."

"Who would lead them to believe this?" the Presatical asked as he abruptly stood. "What fools think I no longer have the power?"

He quickly walked back into the chalet with the second close behind. *What he doesn't know won't hurt me*, the second thought.

As they walked into the receiving room, the Presatical went through the motions of monitoring the reports his Internet watchers handed him. Along with suspect messages broadcast on the web, the Presatical monitored all images and messages emerging from his village.

His computer people had been trained to notice anything unusual or anything directly linked to the Presatical, the savants, or the book. In addition, the Presatical had them monitor all recorded data that ended up on the Internet, such as videos and photos taken in and around the village.

Looking through the pictures a family from Canada had taken, the Presatical felt a shock run through his body when he saw one particular picture.

"Copy this and send it to me," he told one of the computer technicians. "Make ten printed copies and vary the sharpness."

He looked at the photo on the computer screen again. No matter what happened in the whole, wide world, fate seemed to determine that the circle never be broken.

His hand shook slightly as he took the printed copy handed to him as he made his way to his private office. He felt more hopeful than he had in quite a while. He felt he was about to solve a mystery that he had not known about.

As he sat at his desk, he studied the picture. It was so uncanny and so familiar that he had to stop the incredible shivers that threatened to shake his entire body. He knew he was on the right path. And now, he realized why he had been led to Joe Daniels.

He stared at the picture of a blond-haired man smiling into the camera. He compared this picture to the multitude of photographs he had amassed on his quarry. It was definitely Joe Daniels with a bad bleach job.

It was also something else.

The Presatical had known there was something different and something special about Joe Daniels. He had felt there was a connection between the two of them, but he had always thought it was simply a shared connection because of the keys.

He was still in slight shock. He had been that way since he had first seen the picture and, with it, the dawning realization that the connection between Joe Daniels and himself was much, much more.

The dark hair had thrown the Presatical's perceptions and memories off. As he looked at the blonde-haired Joe Daniels in the picture, the Presatical saw the resemblance between Joe and a young woman who had left her home and homeland so many years ago.

That young woman, blue-eyed and blonde-haired, had also left her favorite brother behind. The young boy, who had just lost his father, had been devastated. When he shook the dust off his home several years later, one of the few mementos he took with him had been a faded picture of his favorite sister.

Opening the small box that contained the only remnants of his early life, the Presatical took out a faded photo that had been at the heart of the puzzle he had been trying to solve. He had been almost certain there was a deeper connection between Joe Daniels and himself, but it had been too strange to entertain.

Not anymore.

The connection was there, stronger then he could have ever hoped for or imagined. The small world he thought about was becoming miniscule by the moment. The revelation sent shivers up his spine and at the same time exhilarated him.

The Presatical laid the picture of Joe beside the old, faded picture from so many years before. The truth stared back at him from two sets of similar eyes.

Joe Daniels was the son of his long-lost sister.

4.

It was another beautiful day in Normal.

Vincent Tumin was pleased with the progress the settlement was making. It had been only forty-two days since they had acquired the town and almost everything had gone smoothly. The biggest drawback had been only a minor glitch and it had been resolved within the second week they had been established.

Who would have thought that there would have been an immediate need for critical medical care? A minor first-aid clinic had been one of the first offices up and running, but it had been ill equipped to handle the severe injuries of the man transported to the facility the week before.

Usually, when a protected one had need of intense medical treatment, he or she was sent to a small, guarded community in a remote area of South Dakota. Many of the protected were currently living there and in other remote communities in countries around the world.

The Tarcona community in South Dakota, however, had a greater amount of the most advanced medical and rehabilitation facilities than any of the others. Critical to severe cases were typically sent to Tarcona and then moved to other remote communities across the United States when their injuries improved.

A few residents remained in Tarcona indefinitely when their physical condition was such that they required twenty-four hour, round the clock care. This care included physical therapy or psychiatric help; most of the time it included both.

Evaluations of these residents were conducted every two months. Vincent was on the committee that decided whether the residents would be allowed continued care or whether they were of no further use and would be quietly and humanely put down.

One long-term Tarcona resident had recently awakened from a strange day-walking fugue. Within the past weeks, she had started to remember bits and pieces of her former life.

Part of that former life had involved Joe Daniels.

For that reason, and that reason only, Joe had been brought to Normal instead of to the medical facility at Tarcona. It would have been catastrophic for Joe and the other resident to meet.

Knowing what he knew, Vincent had concluded it would have been disastrous for the two of them to even be within the same radius as each other. The human mind was complex, and so many parts of it were not understood, but Vincent had seen first-hand how emotional connections between people sometimes acted like homing beacons.

He could not take the chance Joe would home in on this particular person, at least, not yet. Because of that, Joe had been brought to Normal and the medical center was quickly enhanced to provide the care he needed. Now, both the community in South Dakota and the town of Normal had superior medical centers.

Vincent knew eventually, both places would become the American epicenters of the Muveed Ursus. The organization had many smaller warehouses and establishments, but only a handful of controlled communities. Now, that number was increasing at a rapid rate.

With the installation of Normal, this brought the Ursus' gated towns to in North America to four hundred and thirty-six. Most of the communities blended into the towns where they were located. Some were actually in the middle of large, metropolitan cities. Every one of the four hundred and thirty-six passed for normal communities. All were discreetly and heavily guarded.

Only a handful of the Ursus knew all of the communities' locations. No one outside of the Ursus suspected anything. Those on the inside would never tell about anything within the organization, willingly or unwillingly. The men and women of the Muveed Ursus were deeply committed to the organization and its principles, and betrayal to them would be like a rare steak to a vegetarian.

Joe Daniels was improving by the hour. His body was

repairing, but Vincent was still unsure about his mind. Joe had made no outward signs that he knew anything beyond the moment he woke up in Normal. Even the laptop they had conveniently left in his room had remained untouched.

Vincent watched as Joe walked around the room. The discreet cameras set up in his room captured his every movement. These cameras were monitored constantly, but Joe had given no sign that he knew who and what he was. At this point, Vincent thought as he turned the camera monitoring back over to the security staff, it is still simply a waiting game.

Unbeknownst to Vincent, Joe was playing the same game. He knew he was being watched because the hairs on the back of his neck had not gone down since he had fully regained his sense of being. He felt sure he had pinpointed the five cameras in his room, but he made a supreme effort to act as though he was unaware of their existence.

All the while, he was beyond anxious to get out. The temptation to get on the laptop that had been placed in his room was great, but he was not stupid – he knew anything he did on the computer would be monitored and tracked.

Joe turned as the door opened and one of his nurses stepped in. Today was the day the mouth guard and the rigid brace on his jaw was coming off. His other injuries were being reevaluated today as well.

As the nurse stepped toward him, a familiar face followed behind. He recognized the woman immediately and somewhat fearfully. The last time he had seen her had been in another life before the chaos began. The last time he had heard anything about her, she had just been widowed and had been on her way out of Joe's old town without a backward glance.

"Hi, Joe," Elizabeth James said. "It's been awhile, hasn't it?"

Seeing his former police partner's wife here was somehow not as much of a shock to Joe as it should have been. As he stared at her, he realized he was becoming immune to surprises.

"Vincent said you were better, so I thought I'd come and see for myself."

Liz twirled a pen between her fingers as she talked. "I guess you figured out Tony and I were part of the whole thing."

She paused and seemed to be lost in thought.

"My parents and Tony's parents were Muveed and so were my grandparents and Tony's. It was in our blood and our heritage," she said as sat down in the chair opposite Joe. "I don't expect you to understand how committed we were to our beliefs, but Tony and I had always known what a risk we were taking."

Again, Liz paused and a sad look crossed her face.

"I just never expected Tony to die the way he did, but I don't blame Frank. He couldn't have known that we were there to protect you."

Liz leaned forward and took Joe's right hand with both of hers. As she held his hand, he felt her index finger trace patterns on his palm. Familiar patterns.

Morse code. Tap. Dash. Tap. Joe's eyes widened slightly as he realized what Liz was trying to tell him.

You are prisoner here forever. I will help. Trust me. They killed my father.

Whatever else she wanted to communicate to Joe was lost when she dropped his hand as a nurse entered the room. Making small talk with the nurse, Liz watched as Joe's mouth guard was removed and he stretched his jaw for the first time in weeks.

"Don't do that too much at first," the nurse cautioned Joe.

Liz looked at Joe as she got up to leave.

"I'll see you again, Joe," she said. "Try to understand, we're all here to help you. We're on your side."

The cameras were surely rolling because Joe knew what Liz was telling him with her mouth was completely opposite of what she had minutes earlier told him with her hand.

What could Joe believe? So many people in his recent past had become other than what they had seemed. The person they had portrayed on the outside was totally different then who they really were. Joe was not sure if he wanted to put all his eggs in the basket with Liz, but he was very sure he wanted to get out of his prison.

After the nurse finished attending him, Joe stretched out on his bed and contemplated his next move. He needed help to get out of the tightly guarded fortress he was trapped in and since Liz was the only person who had offered, Joe knew he would take her up on her help.

Not that he would stick around with her. The only reason she may be offering to help Joe was probably a hidden agenda of her own. And Joe was tired of being on other people's agendas.

Supper came and went. Medical personnel silently went about their business. The cold-eyed man did not visit Joe again that evening, but Joe was sure if anything unusual were to happen, this Muveed puppet would be the first on the scene.

Darkness fell. The night was brilliant with stars. Joe watched the tiny twinkles of brightness through the skylight and wondered, for the umpteenth time, how he had been swallowed up in this mess.

Suddenly, as he was watching the night sky, something blotted out some of the stars. Careful not to show any awareness (he was sure he was being monitored by night vision cameras in the darkened room), he watched as a figure opened one of the panels on the skylight.

The ninja-dark person above Joe was lowering what looked like a rope with a harness attached. The rope stopped a few feet from the skylight and, as Joe watched, it stayed suspended a dozen feet above his head.

As Joe watched the figure making its way down, the lights on his now unused medical monitors flickered and went out. He turned his head and saw that the hallway lights were also out.

The rope dropped quickly. Joe grabbed it and hooked the vest harness around his chest. As soon as he secured it, he gave a gentle tug to whoever it was on the other end of the rope.

Joe had no idea whether he was being hauled up to his freedom or his death, but it was better he at least had a fighting chance to escape the Muveed stronghold.

As he was being pulled up, he briefly thought how glad he was he had been given scrubs to wear to replace the open-backed gown he had had up until a few days before. He was glad nothing personal of his was blowing in the wind.

Of course, partial nudity would not have stopped him from attempting escape. Hell, full nudity would not have stopped him. He would have run bare-assed naked in the middle of the day through a crowded street to get back his freedom.

He had almost made it to the top of the skylight when a gloved hand reached down to pull him up. Grasping the hand and the edge of the opened skylight panel, Joe hoisted himself up and over.

"Quiet," Liz whispered as Joe sat beside her. She quickly gathered the rope and closed the open panel. For all intents and purposes, it would seem Joe had disappeared from a locked room, like a Hitchcock movie.

Slipping over the side of the domed skylight, Joe and Liz shimmied fifteen feet down a pipe anchored to the building. Putting a finger to her lips when they touched ground, Liz took Joe's hand and led him close to the interconnecting buildings.

The lights were still out. As they scurried quickly along the walls, Joe could see people quietly and urgently running all over the place.

"We have to get out of here before they get the power back on," Liz whispered as they came to the last building. Joe could see the guardhouse guarding the entrance into town about fifty yards away. As they rounded the corner of that last building, Liz walked straight into one of her superiors.

"You're not scheduled to come back until Friday," the man said. "Why are you here, Liz?"

He paused as he looked at her attire. "You need to come

with me," he said to her. As he grabbed Liz by the arm, he briefly felt a hard, sinewy arm encircle his neck before he lost consciousness.

His neck snapped as the grip around it tightened and twisted the man's head sharply up toward the heavens.

Joe's right arm was working just fine, he thought as he lowered the body to the ground. He had never used the one-arm death grip that Sgt. Matters had shown him until now.

Joe looked at Liz and said hoarsely, "We need to hide him."

The last building was used for storage. As they dragged the body inside, Joe could barely make out a group of large pipes in the dark. He motioned Liz to help him stuff the body inside.

Since there had been no blood, they did not have to worry about someone following a trail and discovering the corpse. In fact, it might be several days before someone traced the smell of decomposition.

"What now?" Joe asked.

Liz looked at the glowing face of her watch. "We have three minutes and twenty-two seconds before they get the power back on. We'll have to run for it."

As they jogged out of the building, Liz whispered to Joe, "There's an electrical field around the outskirts of town. We have to get past it before the power's back on. I tripped the main power grid and all four of the backups, but if someone figures out what I did, they could get power back up in seconds."

Liz looked at Joe as they rounded the back of the last building. "Once you start running, don't stop for anything. If we get separated, there's a truck with keys and a change of clothes in it for you two miles north. It's parked under brush at the foot of the only hill in that direction."

The open field behind the building screamed freedom to Joe. Itching to get out of Dodge, Joe tempered himself and waited for the woman he had partially entrusted his life with to give a signal to start running like a hellhound.

Liz put an arm out in front of Joe's chest. "Stop," she

barely whispered.

She listened to the sounds around her and pulled out a pair night-vision goggles. Even without infrared help, Joe could make out the landscape glowing slightly from the cloudy moonlight.

Tapping Joe's chest, Liz pointed to the west and held up two fingers, pointed outward, and held up three fingers. If they had run in that direction, they would have tripped into two perimeter guards three hundred yards ahead.

Thankfully, the guards were looking in the wrong direction and had not spotted Joe and Liz. At least, for now.

Quietly, the pair of escapees changed course and lit out across the field.

The hard rocky ground cut into Joe's bare feet, but it did not slow him down. He had grown used to pain lately, so this was simply a minor inconvenience.

Running across the open field, Joe had no idea where the actual perimeter was located. For all he knew, he had already passed it, but, then again, maybe it was further ahead. He just did not want to come into a nasty shock if the power went on before he could cross over.

To be captured again would have been the end of him. He knew that if they caught him, he would be shackled and bound with absolutely no chance of freedom ever again.

This thought gave him an extra burst of energy and helped put his aching ribs and feet out of his mind.

Like wild banshees, Liz and Joe ran until they came to a small gravel road. Panting and wheezing as they paused, Joe felt like his lungs were going to burst.

"Let's go," Liz gasped in between gulping for air. "We can't stop."

Trudging ahead, Liz turned and motioned Joe to keep up. Joe's feet were killing him, but the prospect of hanging around was worse.

As they came to the bottom of the hill, Liz quickly pulled the leafy covering off the hidden non-descript pick-up truck. As they jumped in the front seat, Joe felt the ground tremble slightly and saw the darkened Muveed town's light come on for a millisecond before parts of the place rocked with an explosion.

Joe looked at Liz and she looked back at him as she started the truck. "I left them a little present."

Liz was quickly turning into Joe's kind of woman.

"Look in that bag by your feet. I put some clothes in there for you to change into." Liz grabbed two water bottles from under her seat. "Here," she said, still panting slightly from their run as she handed Joe the water.

Joe swallowed almost all of the water in one gulp. It cooled his parched and aching throat, but at the same time, it burned like hell. Clearing his throat, Joe's voice did not sound as gravelly as it had fifteen minutes before.

"Thanks," he croaked as Liz floored the accelerator.

He opened the bag by his feet and pulled out a pair of jeans and a black t-shirt. Suppressing a shudder, he remembered this was identical to what he had had on when he had been arrested for the alleged murder of his alleged wife.

In the cramped front seat, somehow Joe managed to slip the jeans and shirt on without giving Liz a full-monty show. He winced as he put socks and a pair of boots on his shredded feet.

Liz noticed his quiet pain. "I'll take care of your feet when we get to my safe house. But, before we can go any further, there's something I have to do," she said as she turned down a small paved road and stopped the truck.

Taking Joe's left arm, Liz felt along the inside until she came to an almost imperceptible bump. Pulling a sterile-sealed scalpel out of the glove compartment, she made a tiny cut by the light of a flashlight she had handed Joe to hold.

"You know what this is, don't you?"

Joe simply nodded. They had managed to plant a gol, a tiny tracking device, underneath his skin.

"That's the one I can see," she said as she flicked it outside. "If they did the ingestible one, there's a way to short-circuit it, but I can't do that here."

Joe shook his head. "They'll track me. If there's any left,

we've gotta get them out of me now."

"Can't do it here," Liz paused. "Unless you want me to hook your gonads up to the truck battery."

Joe shook his head again. "I'll wait."

Pulling back onto the road, the rebels put miles and miles between them and the people who were coming after them.

Driving all night and day, they shared shifts at the wheel. Neither could sleep when it was not their time to drive. They were both on high alert.

After hundreds of miles on the road, they finally pulled into Liz's safe house. As Liz unlocked the gate, Joe read a small, hand-carved inscription on one of the posts.

Templum Damno.

Sanctuary of the Damned.

5.

As soon as they entered the house, Liz took a hand-held scanner and ran it up and down Joe's body.

"Nothing. If you'd had another transmitter, it would have shown up on the scanner."

Liz motioned him to sit down on the couch as she went into the kitchen. Joe looked around at the cluttered cottage and the first thing he noticed was a large picture of a man in military regalia.

Joe's heart skipped a beat and he felt his face pale as he stared at the portrait on the wall. Joe never knew the man had a family. He had never talked about a life outside of the branch of service to which he had committed his life.

Liz was Sergeant Robert Matter's daughter.

He was dead.

And he had been Muveed Ursus.

Coming out a few minutes later with a small tub, Liz set the water on the floor in front of Joe. Taking his boots off, Liz gently removed the blood-caked socks stuck to Joe's feet.

Still stunned, Joe looked at Liz, and as she met his eyes, she nodded and said, "Now you know. He was my father."

Liz continued to bathe Joe's feet, but Joe's numb mind had extended to his body and he no longer felt the pain in the soles of his feet.

"He was Muveed," Joe stated.

"Yeah. But he was more loyal to his combat 'boys' than he was to Muveed. When he tried to help you, he used channels in Muveed. They told me that was the last straw."

As she continued to bathe his feet, Liz's eyes took on a sad, faraway look. "He was a good man and he just wanted to make everything right. He had the highest sense of fairness and that's what got him killed.

"My dad told me that tagline, an army of one, was wrong. He believed the army, or any of the other military branches, was strongest when individuals came together as a group of independent thinkers with a common goal. That's what he was trying to teach you guys."

"I'm sorry," Joe said as he touched Liz's shoulder.

Liz looked up at him and, with hard eyes, said, "I watched him die. They said it was a test of my loyalty to the Muveed Ursus." As her eyes started to fill, she went on, "He had told me he would die someday because his beliefs conflicted with Muveed. He was so matter of fact about it."

The tears never spilled and Liz's eyes hardened again. "I can't bring them all down by myself, but I'll take out as many as I can before they get me."

Pushing her sleeves up, Joe noticed a large, stitched cut on Liz's right arm. Noticing his look, Liz explained, "Being part of covert ops, I had a transmitter and a receiver." Looking at the long cut, Liz continued, "It took a little more exploring to get mine out, but they're gone now," she said with a shrug as she put antibiotic ointment on Joe's feet and wrapped them with bandages.

Joe shook his head. "Were you a biker in a former life, 'cause you are one tough mama."

Liz laughed. "Nah. I'm just a mean bitch with a vendetta."

Exhaustion hit both of them at the same time. With a mumbled good night, Joe lay back on the couch and was asleep before his head hit the throw pillow.

***

Pain.

The day after arriving at Liz's safe house, Joe woke to aches and pains from the top of his head to the bottom of his feet. The adrenaline rush he had had the day before had quickly worn off and a bastard load of pain was coursing through his body.

Groaning, Joe eased himself off the couch and limped toward the bathroom. After taking care of business, Joe walked into the kitchen in time to see Liz whirl around as a bullet whizzed past her head.

As they both crab-crawled along the floor, Liz reached for a black box beside the refrigerator. "When I hit this, we're gonna drop into the basement."

Handing Joe a set of keys, Liz continued: "There's a tunnel that'll lead you to a creek. Follow the creek about a half-mile upstream until it makes a bend. Go up the gravel road to your left and there's a Jeep parked about a hundred feet up."

Liz hit the black-box buttons. Bombs exploded in a circumference around the Templum Damno and at the same instance, the kitchen floor dropped out from underneath them.

As they plunged into the basement, Joe was not sure if the screams he was hearing were his and Liz's or if they were coming from outside.

Not bothering to dust fragments of wood away, they both raced toward the series of tunnels lit by phosphorous stones common to the area. As they ran, Liz told him, "They tracked us and I don't know how. I never came here after they implanted the trackers in my arm."

For the first time since Joe had been on the lam with Liz, she looked scared. "We've got to split up." She pointed to her left and told Joe, "You go that way."

She paused for a second before continuing, "I'll meet you at the Jackson White Park in Middleton, Iowa, tomorrow. Meet me in the morning along the trail at the marker for the thousand-year oak."

As another explosion rocked the earth around them, Liz screamed at Joe, "Go!" as she took off down an opposite tunnel.

Joe ran even faster than he had the night of his escape from Normal. As adrenaline kicked in, he was able to briefly ignore the pain in his feet. But, not for long.

Cursing each time his feet hit the ground, he wished he had had time to slip some boots on so he would not be tearing his feet up again.

Time, though, was not on his side. First, he had escaped the Muveed city-fortress barefoot and in scrubs, now he was escaping them again in bare feet. At least he had his jeans and a shirt on.

As he ran, a thought repeated itself over and over in his head: the Muveed had had plenty of time to tamper with his body while he was unconscious. If they had planted a tracking device inside of him, they would be able to find him no matter where he hid.

Liz had checked with a scanner, but what if it was a tracker that could not be detected? If that was the case, he was better off dead.

Coming out of the tunnel, he looked back and saw the woods on fire where Liz's house had been.

Good. He hoped the demolition dame's bombs had taken out an entire unit of Muveed.

Following the stream like Liz had told him, he quickly came to the bend and followed the road to the left. The Jeep was exactly where she had told him it would be.

Surprisingly, there was a bag in the Jeep containing two sets of clothes, socks, boots, and sneakers, along with a first aid kit, a dozen bottles of water, an assortment of military-style rations, five hundred dollars in cash, and a very illegally modified Glock 18.

That girl was better than any Boy Scout Joe had ever known.

Joe popped the clutch and took off. As he drove along the dirt road parallel to the creek, he kept track of how many miles he was putting between himself and Templum Damno. Or, he thought, it should be called Templum Fatum, Sanctuary of Doom.

After the gravel road turned into a paved highway, Joe's danger meter kicked in. Every vehicle that passed him or stayed behind him for longer than a few minutes became suspect.

Crossing into Iowa that afternoon, Joe stopped at the Welcome Center to grab a map. He was only about two hours from Middleton.

Sitting in the Jeep as he studied the map, he glanced up as group of black sedans pulled in. He knew who they were without even seeing the bear emblem on the windshield.

Muveed must be scouting every place along the interstate looking for him. Thank God, he had not even asked the lady at the Welcome Center where to find Middleton. All he had asked for was a map.

Watching through his sunglasses, he waited until two cars down the row from him were backing out before he put the Jeep in reverse. He wanted to blend with a convoy of vehicles; he could not afford to stand out from the crowd.

It took him less than two hours to drive through Middleton. He kept going until he had put a hundred miles between himself and the town.

Stopping at a slightly dilapidated roadside motel, Joe used cash to pay for his room. When the desk clerk asked for an ID, Joe told her he did not have one. No problem, apparently, as long as you forked over a hundred dollars for a deposit.

After Joe propped a chair against the doorknob, he laid his G18 on the table beside the bed and flipped the fire-control selector switch from semi to fully automatic. If anyone tried to force their way into Joe's room, that unfortunate person would be cut in half by a rake of bullets fired at 1400 rpm's.

Joe's sleep was fitful, partially from the events of the last few days and partially from his aches and pains. Waking the next morning before the sun came up, Joe still felt incredibly tired. Splashing cold water on his face, he dressed, and headed out the door.

The Jackson White Park was a few miles south of Middleton. Joe parked the Jeep on what looked like an unused dirt road about a half mile away and walked through a cluster of dense woods back toward the park.

Coming to a service road for park employees, he followed it until it merged into an asphalted road. Keeping close to the trees, Joe found the trail the public used to view the many beautiful plants and trees.

Any other time he would have enjoyed the nature walk. Now, he was on a mission to find a geriatric oak tree.

Within ten minutes, he had found the tree. Stepping off the trail, Joe hunkered down on the sore balls of his feet and waited.

Liz showed up seventy-five minutes later.

Casually looking around, Liz did not see Joe as he came up behind her. When she turned at his touch, she did not bat an eye.

"Remember the guy that stopped me and tried to take me in? He tapped me with a gripper ghoul when he touched my arm. I never changed clothes. It was my fault they found us. They tracked me after I left the safe house. It didn't hit me the tracker was on me until I realized that was why I couldn't shake Muveed off my tail."

Liz looked uncomfortable as she continued. "I made some truckers very happy when I stripped and threw my clothes out the window."

Joe grinned at Liz's discomfort. "I guess you found some more clothes."

"Yeah. On a clothesline right across state line."

Both turned as they heard voices coming toward them. "Let's get off the trail," Joe suggested.

Moving deeper into the wilder part of the woods, Joe did not have to help Liz at all. He blamed his inability to keep up with her on his soreness, but he really thought, and this was hard to admit to himself, that Liz was a better soldier than he was.

After they found a place deep in the woods with a vantage point where they could see in all directions, they sat on the ground. Liz put a finger to her lips as Joe opened his mouth.

Watching as she took a camouflage cloth out of the backpack she was wearing, Joe thought she looked more like a college student than an ops bomb specialist.

Within a minute, the camouflage cloth was above their heads.

"I think we have enough cover," Joe said.

"It's not for cover, ass," Liz told him. "Look close at the cloth."

As Joe looked closer as the camouflage cloth, he saw tiny metallic threads running all through the fabric. "It's a disrupter, isn't it?"

"Yeah. We're good from direct over head surveillance and there's enough spit in the wires to garble any directional shit. Courtesy of Muveed."

"Question: why didn't your dad know about the Presatical?"

"I didn't know about that abomination until Dad told me. Dad was Muveed, but only a few top Muveed know about sensitive stuff like that. Dad pretty much figured a lot out on his own.

"He knew he was up against road's end when he started helping you and the rest of your unit. It did not matter that he was fifth generation Muveed 'cause Dad was big on loyalty to the ones who need you the most."

"I'm really sorry, Liz. So many people have been hurt because of me."

Liz backhanded Joe on the face. Hard.

"Do you really think you're so important that people died for you? Get over the Jesus complex, shithead. People died because Muveed and the Presatical are trying to keep their control over the world.

"You're a pawn with something they both want – your memories. I don't want to know if you still have those memories – I don't care, except for the fact that I'll shoot you in the head before I'd let anyone else take you alive."

Joe looked at Liz with his head slightly cocked. "That's oddly comforting in a scary way."

"I'm serious. You may or may not have these memories everybody's after. If you don't, good for you, because, if you do, I think they're going to be more of a burden than anything else you've had to deal with."

"Is Beanie alive?" Joe asked.

"Your wife?" Liz paused. "I really don't know. I do know they have someone connected to you at one of the Muveed strongholds, but I don't know who it is or which one he or she's at. Finding people was never my strong point. Blowing them up's more my speed."

Joe laughed and laughed harder when Liz looked at him in puzzlement. "What's so funny?"

"Look," Joe said, "don't take this the wrong way, but you look way too young to be a demolitions expert. What are you? Seventeen?"

Joe grinned as Liz turned a little red. "Piss off," she told him.

As they sat quietly, Joe turned to Liz and asked, "What do we do now?"

"That's up to you," she replied. "We can hunker down and let some of the shit blow over; that might take a few years or decades. We can take out as many strongholds as we can before they kill us. We can pop over to see the Presatical, since you seem to know where to find him, and maybe you can have a heart-to-heart with him."

Liz paused. "It's your decision, Joe. I'll be with you as long as I'm alive and you need me. When Dad was helping you, he told me you were a keeper, and, believe me, most people were pure rubbish to Dad. He saw something in you. I think he believed you would make a difference in the world. He had never been this keen on helping someone as he was with you."

Joe quietly listened and, as he listened, he realized that everything Sarge had ever done for him had been preparing him for this moment of epiphany.

Could one man make a difference? Obviously, one man could since the Presatical was living proof of that.

But could one man named Joe make a difference?

He did not know, but he sure as hell was going to try.

After a few moments of quiet, Joe turned to Liz and smiled as he stood up and held out his hand to help her up.

"Let's go catch us a whale."

6.

On the road, again.

That night, they crossed the Iowa state line into South Dakota and headed north toward a part of the country that was still untamed and undeveloped. It would be the perfect place to recoup and do some serious strategic planning.

Liz had ditched her vehicle somewhere along the way and they were riding in an older model pickup truck she had jacked from the back of a used car lot. From the outside, Liz and Joe looked like a married couple, worn down by a hard life.

Both were haggard, and fatigue made them both look like they were on the verge of passing out. It had been a hard couple of days for the pair as they went from escape to escape to escape.

It was even harder for Joe; he had been on the go for the better part of a year. Even though his military training had prepared him to be on the alert for the enemy at all times, it had never prepared him to be on the alert for foe and so-called friend alike.

Pulling into an all-night truck stop, Liz and Joe sat in the truck for an hour while they scouted the place out. When they finally went in, they still did not feel safe.

Sitting in a booth with their backs to the wall, they ordered and quickly ate their food without saying a word to each other. To anyone paying attention, they really did look like a couple who had been together for too long and were just going through the motions of a stale marriage.

Leaving the truck stop, they noticed the weather had already turned colder. In addition to extra clothes for Joe, Liz had somehow found some winter gear for both of them.

With admiration, Joe realized Liz was a very resourceful woman and one that would be handy to have on his side.

But there was no spark of love for her. Admiration, a large degree of trust, and a forced camaraderie, but no love. Joe's heart was beating still, but it beat for only one woman.

Joe would go to the pits of hell and fight Satan himself to avenge his wife. More than love, he felt an enormous amount of guilt. It was because of him that Beanie had been dragged into the whole fucking mess.

Dawn came slowly as they traveled deserted roads. The place Liz was headed toward was a defunct survivalist's camp that she had come across when she had been sent to find a target in the northwestern part of North Dakota.

From that place, she had found a map to a smaller survivalist's camp in the Badlands of North Dakota. Veering from her intended target, she made a quick sweep of the area and tucked the location in the back of her mind.

Even during her most intense dedication to Muveed, a part of her was planning an eventual escape. Just like her own father, she had never given herself completely to the organization. Her father had been a man among men, and had never hidden behind anything or anyone.

They would be safe there, for awhile. Since the Muveed were everywhere, they would not be safe forever. Like Gypsies, they would have to move from place to place. In a way, Liz liked the thought – it reminded her of her childhood, living in a different place every year or so when her father was assigned to a new base.

About four o'clock that afternoon, Liz pulled off the road onto a nearly invisible path running against the side of a huge rock formation. As Joe looked on, he watched as Liz continued to follow the formation.

When she turned toward the formation itself, and seemed intent on running head-on into the side of the huge rock, Joe made a motion to grab the wheel.

Reacting instinctively, Liz immediately drew her gun and pointed it at Joe and just as immediately withdrew it.

"Watch," she said, as she drove straight toward the rock.

Hoping like hell the airbags worked in the old truck, Joe had no choice but to watch.

But what he saw amazed him.

He never saw the opening in the rock, but it was there. They passed through it without mishap and were inside the formation the rock encircled.

"Sorry about the gun," Liz sheepishly said after they passed through the naturally camouflaged opening. "It's habit."

"Okay, now what in the world was that?" Joe asked.

"It's called 'hunahas kanitis' and it's the most amazing optical allusion in the world. I can't even begin to explain it because I have no idea how it works. I just know that it means 'disappearing rock' and the Akira tribe used it when they were at war to confuse their enemies.

"The kicker is that this is just one of about two hundred hunahas kanitas that are supposed to be here in the Badlands. I got the info from a historian at Fort Berthold when I was researching where this camp was because I couldn't see anywhere on a map about how to get to it."

Liz stopped the truck in front of a large rock.

As she got out and walked toward the rock, she told Joe, who had also gotten out, "Now, this is just a plain Hollywood stage set." Pushing the rock away with one hand, Joe understood what she meant.

"Papier-mâché," Liz laughed.

Liz moved the tuck to a concealed area and Joe walked through the opening into a small encampment that reminded him of the hundreds of military and guerilla camps he had seen and sometimes stayed in. Oddly, he felt right at home.

"This is it," Liz said. "We've got enough provisions to feed us for years. But most of all, it's probably the safest place on Earth for us, right now. You see those silver streaks at the top of the formation?"

Joe looked to where Liz was pointing and saw what seemed to be real silver stripes running alongside the rocks.

"When I first came here, I found out those streaks are some type of silver that fucks up a radio signal. And a satellite signal, too. The only signal that it doesn't mess up is a ham radio."

Liz looked a little embarrassed as she started pulling out the few items in the truck. "But I forgot the ham radio," she stated as Joe stepped over to help.

Stopping, Joe put his hand on Liz's shoulder and said, "Thank you for saving me. You've done so much in such a short time and you've given me much more than I had." He paused. "You gave me back my freedom." He patted her shoulder. "Thank you."

After unloading their meager belongings, the pair went into the largest of the camps and set it to order. Although it looked like it had been years since anyone had been in the cabin, Joe was holding out hope that everything was in working order.

A storage shed behind the cabin had enough fuel to keep the generator running day and night. Once Joe got the generator started, he was a little amazed that the lights, refrigerator, and stove worked.

Liz and Joe quickly cleaned the place and got everything organized. Once they settled in, they were able to relax for the first time since their ordeal had started. Although they were as safe as possible for the moment, Joe was still on "high alert." He felt that any moment, someone would find them, and he was scared that it would be an enemy.

They settled into a routine: mornings were spent securing their hideout, afternoons were spent going over and sharing knowledge about the people and organizations they were facing, and evenings were for recouping. Joe especially needed the evenings: his body was not recovering as fast as it had when he was younger and numerous aches and pains that had not been there before were making him realize that growing older was a bitch.

Even though he was slower in healing, he pursued a punishing daily regimen of exercising that rivaled anything he had had to do in the military. Liz was impressed by his commitment, which she told him, and a little unnerved by his obsession with bulking up, which she did not tell him. She did not want to disillusion him by telling him that he-man muscles wouldn't stop a bullet or a thrown knife.

During their time together at the camp, Liz talked about her father and Joe learned that Liz had a brother who had been missing for several years. Liz teared up when she talked about her sibling.

"Ricky was just a year older than me," she told Joe one evening. "We grew up at my grandmother's after my mom died. I had just turned eight and Ricky was nine. Dad was still stationed at Fort Adams and was in the middle of transferring closer to Me-maw's so he could be around more."

Taking a sip of instant coffee, Liz continued. "It was me and Ricky for the longest time. Dad would come home as much as he could, but it was hard for him to get leave, because of the Gulf War and all.

"Me-maw did the best she could with us," Liz said with a small smile. "She just wasn't used to kids after so many years. Ricky and I got away with most everything when Dad wasn't there."

Liz's smile disappeared as she went on. "I was sixteen when Ricky disappeared." She paused and Joe saw a faraway look in her eyes. "When I got home from school, Me-maw told me Ricky had skipped classes and she was going to tear his hide up when he came home. When he didn't come home that evening, or the next day, or the next, Me-maw called Dad."

A single tear escaped and trailed down Liz's face. She wiped it away and Joe saw her face harden as she told him more. "Years later, Dad told me he suspected Muveed, but could never prove it. He felt if it was Muveed, and he was ninety percent certain it was, then it was a punishment for his questioning something that had happened after some of his military 'boys' had been on a mission."

She looked at Joe and Joe intuitively knew which mission she was talking about.

"It was when we found the keys, wasn't it?" he asked. "Muveed knew what the keys were and who we were way before the Presatical even knew the damned things were missing, didn't they?"

"Yeah," Liz replied, "but they didn't find out from my dad. You guys were as important to him as his own family and he protected you just like he tried to protect me and my brother.

"Dad told me he believed they had watchers on the vault at all times and when the keys were stolen, the watchers followed them until you and your buddies threw them in the fire. After that, Muveed kept an eye on everyone involved.

"At that time, Muveed was still practicing more of a watchful involvement than what they're doing right now. They've evolved in the past decade into something more frightening than the Presatical: they've become a power without a center."

Joe felt a chill as it dawned on him that his enemies were more insidious than he could have imagined. The Muveed had had him under surveillance for a long, long time and he had not been aware of their presence until all the shit hit the fan when Beanie had the accident.

It was even worse to think either they were connected to Beanie's accident or they simply watched without lifting a hand as horrible things happened to Joe and the people around him.

How much of everyone's daily lives were the Muveed entangled in? The answer Joe was forming boggled his mind. If they had their slimy tentacles into every facet of society, the Muveed organization was more powerful than anything anyone could every have imagined.

To think that they were involved in the things that had happened to Joe made him madder than hell. Supposedly a watch-dog group, they were more like the mean boy whispering malicious things into the school bully's ear, making him do things he might not normally have had the wits to do.

The Muveed were the ultimate shit stirrers.

Everyone involved with the Muveed, whether by choice or unintentionally, paid a price. A son gone missing, a wife crushed in an accident, a good friend turned traitor. The more he thought about them all, the more pissed Joe got.

As he looked at Liz, the hard shell of inhumanness that suddenly came over Joe's face took her aback. It was the same callous look she had seen a few times before on the face of Muveed's unofficial leader, the cold-eyed man.

Growing up tough, having a drill sergeant for a father, and being trained by the world's most ruthless organization, Liz did not frighten easily, but the look on Joe's face made her think that, under the right circumstances, he would cut someone's heart out with a dull rock and never think twice about it.

At that very moment, she definitely wanted him on her side down whatever dark path they were destined to travel.

Their routine never wavered the three weeks they were in the camp. They had more than enough provisions to last a few years, so they never went into the town located a few miles away.

Life was not slow at the camp. Since the hideout was as secure as it was going to get, most of their waking hours were spent bulking up and planning. Joe was all for jumping headlong into the fray that was ultimately brewing between the Presatical and the Muveed. But, Liz knew Muveed much better than Joe; they would be expecting the pair of rebels to do just that.

Trying to convince Joe that patience and caution were their best weapons was a daunting task for Liz. Although fairly easy-going, Joe was turning out be as stubborn as a cat on a leash. The scales tipped in Liz's favor when she told Joe, in no uncertain terms, that either Muveed or the Presatical would capture both of them if they jumped in without a net and then neither of them would ever see the sun again.

The clincher was when Liz told Joe that if he were captured, both of those horrible organizations would go on and on with no one to stop them. Stopping Muveed and the Presatical were on an even par with having his revenge for the horrible things both evil entities had done to Joe and to those close to Joe.

Joe was finally convinced that patience and caution, traits he used to have, were the elements he and Liz would need to defeat the hellhounds.

The weeks they were in the camp were isolated. They

had no contact with the outside world. At all.

There was no way they could know that while they were in their safe retreat, the world had fallen deeper into chaos and, for quite a few people, it seemed as though the gates of hell had opened and Armageddon was upon them.

7.

Earth was under siege.

The hounds of war had been loosed and the entire world was preparing for battle. Nations were organizing their military forces to wage war against other nations, countries were already battling their neighbors, and in some areas, even cities were arming themselves against the villages close to them. Only people who were living in caves were unaffected by the changes across all lands.

The most telling sign came when neutral Switzerland entered the fray. Over the past decade, the Swiss Army had downgraded from over half a million to less than one hundred thousand active conscripts or a little less than one percent of the population.

Once the chaos began, the Swiss Army bulked up its numbers tenfold. The irony was they were doing this by drawing on ordinary Swiss citizens who, for the most part, had never picked up anything more lethal than a sharpened pencil.

Without the knowledge of the secluded and unreachable Presatical, the center was unraveling. Nations who had previously supported and protected Switzerland were gathering at that nation's borders and the Swiss were quick to morph from lambs to lions.

There was no war tally. While each nation kept an unofficial scorecard, it had always been expressly forbidden to document the count. Any nation discovered keeping an official record of man and land count was quickly suppressed by the Book of the Deceived's coalition of nations. Suppressed, conquered, and divided.

Very few nations were willing to risk losing their power over simple bookkeeping. Their main concern was governing and protecting their own lands, and, of course, sharing in the spoils of whichever war was going on at the time. Anyway, that was the Presatical's only job; all he had to do was keep a fair measure of man and land.

With the Presatical nowhere to be found for the past few months, however, each nation in the Deceived's coalition had become self-sustaining, totalitarian, and lethally defensive. Power nations closed borders and began making their own decisions about war and peace, albeit, mostly on the war side. None were willing to negotiate since they only had a vague idea of where they stood in the war tally.

Those few nations outside of the coalition were quickly overcome. Out of control power nations brutally gobbled up their weaker neighbors and within a few weeks, world geography changed dramatically.

The United States kicked into high gear, recalling overseas troops and mobilizing for northern and southern invasions, officially called "protective domicile measures." Any and all means of force were sanctioned by the federal government. A large majority of the population, still reeling from terrorist attacks on U. S. soil, supported these actions.

The Canadian government looked across its southern border and very quickly acquiesced to the American military supremacy. The rapidity the U. S. set up its own government in Canada testified to a plan which had been in place for decades. Within a matter of days, Canada became a territory of the new United States of the Americas.

Since the United Mexican States had already been on its way to an official alliance with the United States, the total takeover of Mexico was relatively easy. A United States government body backed by the military was placed in each of the former federation's thirty-one states and its one federal district. The few places holding out were bombed into submission and the people who would not swear an allegiance to the United States of the Americas were executed.

South America was an entirely different story. Fiercely independent and historically revolutionary, South America, with Brazil as the leading military power, did not roll over easily for the new United States. Because time was of the essence, the US military did not hesitate to threaten atomic bombing, since they would rather lose the people and land of

South America than to have it fall into the hands of another superpower.

But, even the threat of a Hiroshima type bombing did not scare the South Americans. It was not until the military used a-bombs on Cuba (who had also declined to be enveloped in the new regime) and the entire land was laid waste that South America changed its mind. When the stench of rotting, burnt corpses reached northern Venezuela and Columbia, Brazil decided it would be better for South America to join the new United States of the Americas than to face annihilation.

The main South American guerilla holdouts were located in Bolivia and the U S military lost no time in making life miserable for the rebels. Dork bombs, sweet peas, and crab junkets were dropped on suspected rebel camps with great accuracy. These dirty weapons full of airborne chemicals and diseases from the unlocked cabinets of the CDC quickly made enlisting with the United States far more attractive than watching one's body parts develop weeping sores before falling off at the bone.

And back at home base? The good old U S of A became a military state overnight. The few anti-military groups who believed peace and openness would rule the day were given a choice: prepare to fight or die. These misguided few who actually thought positive passive actions would save the world from the sliding into global war were quickly educated about the realities of the new world.

Federally sanctioned militias sprang up in every town across the continental United States. From the larger metropolitan cities down to tiny secluded hamlets, men and women eagerly enlisted to fight to protect their way of life. Scared by federal government by the thought of becoming pawns or slaves to foreign powers, ordinary citizens took up arms and swore an allegiance to protect at all costs the new United States of the Americas.

Some states and communities eagerly pledged to defend their new country. Texas became the new center of government, as the District of Columbia was deemed too laxly protected and, unofficially, too anti-military.

Texas, on the other hand, was home to the most legal guns per citizen in the country. Homes with guns were the norm and Texans were encouraged to defend their turf. The crime rate for violent crimes in Texas was one of the lowest in the country. Criminals thought twice before breaking into a home or attempting to rob a Texan since the odds of the criminal being shot were much higher in Texas than anywhere else in the country.

So, for a country becoming a military state, Texas was the most logical place to seat the new military government. Texans, for their part, welcomed the chance to holster their weapons openly. Although Texas had long unofficially rewarded their citizens for taking the law into their own hands, now they could openly dare reprobates and degenerates to cross the line.

Lawlessness was not tolerated. Violent crimes against allegiance-sworn citizens of the new republic were dealt with swiftly and lethally. The new United States of the Americas treasured each legally gun-toting citizen. These paramilitary groups would be called upon to defend the territories along with the regular military when, not if, other super powers tried to invade the country.

For this reason, each sworn citizen was granted the right to use vigilante justice with no repercussions. In essence, every citizen became a military nucleus of one.

Crime rates plummeted to an all time low. Once thieves learned they would be either shot dead at the scene of the crime or pursued and then shot dead by vigilantes, they decided to either go underground or mend their ways.

A new temporary department in this new government was in charge of the prisons. Non-violent prisoners were given the choice of serving their sentences in work camps or enlisting in the military. Violent criminals who had not taken a life were sent to work camps; some exceptions were made depending on the crime committed and these were sent to serve in the military.

Murderers, rapists, molesters, and torturers had their life

sentences commuted to death. Within two weeks, all prisoners on death row were executed; no appeals were heard.

Prisons were transformed into work camps or military bases. The entire nation's prison population was down to zero. Criminals who were caught were either shot on the spot or sentenced by a judge to a work camp within hours of committing their crimes.

People still went about their business, working and shopping, attending church, vacationing, but everything was now done with a gun or two and a new sense of security in one's self and one's country.

For the majority of the population, handling unfamiliar weapons proved easier than was first thought possible. Shooting lessons became mandatory, whether the citizen kept a gun or not. Instruction was taught by either the local police department or military base, or, in some cases, by neighborhood crime watch organizations.

For the first in history, the entire federation of the Americas was united against a common enemy. Because this threat affected every single person, the government reinforced the concept of strength in numbers.

Once the borders surrounding the United States of the Americas were secured and guarded with diligence by the military and the citizen militia, the American conquistadors next looked to the east.

Greenland had always been considered a vast, frozen wasteland, but upon second look during this time of chaos, Greenland took on a special importance to the States. Because of its geographic location and size, it could become one of the first buffers from foreign attacks against the United States.

The only problem was wresting it from the French.

Once the chaos had started, Germany and France joined forces, and overtook Denmark, along with several smaller European countries. Since France had the stronger maritime force, they began to mobilize to guard German and French territories in the Atlantic.

Avoiding the English coastline, the first French fleet arrived on the independent republic of Iceland's coastline within the second week of world chaos. Claiming the land in the name of the French/German coalition came at a cost: while France had maritime experience, the Icelanders ruled the waters around their homeland.

Ultimately, France's weaponry won the short battle in swift and bloody order.

Because of the time France spent securing Iceland, their descent upon Greenland was delayed enough for the new United States of the Americas to establish an enormous military presence on land and water.

Greenlanders welcomed the States. Living mostly on the coastlines because of the frozen interior, the citizens of Greenland were both strong in coastal defense because of the nature of their land and weak at the same time because there was nowhere to run if a battle turned sour.

Greenlanders were quick to realize their defenseless position put them at risk between American and European superpowers. Although the country's natives valued their independence, they knew dependency on any European country other than Denmark would be intolerable. Greenland decided it was better for them to have the partial freedom under the Americans than to have little or no freedom under Europe. To have the full might of the States naval forces was a relief to the isolated country.

By the time France finished its bloody conquest of Iceland and headed toward Greenland, the States' naval and marine forces were firmly entrenched on land and in the territorial waters surrounding the large island. It only took the sinking of two of France's warships to turn the short-lived battle into a win for the States.

Three hundred and seven French seamen died that day. American casualties: zero.

Elsewhere in the world, China battled Russia and Saudi Arabia, the newest superpower alliance, for dominance in Eastern Europe. The entire southeastern section of Asia consisting of India, Cambodia, Vietnam, the Koreas, Japan,

Indonesia, and the Philippines was under Chinese conquest rule.

Russia was surprisingly able to wrest Mongolia away from Chinese dominance, at least for the moment. The northeastern territories of China, however, became a major battleground between the two countries.

On the western front, China battled Saudi Arabia for control of Pakistan and Afghanistan. Turkey, Iran, Egypt, and ten of the northernmost states of Africa had already fallen under the Saudi rule in the first week of the chaos. Day by day, the Saudis added smaller African states to its military rule.

In a surprise move, the black and white South Afrikaners put aside their cultural and political differences to organize and amass a huge military force to secure the lower half of the African continent.

In another equally surprising move during the second week of the chaos, this new African force was able to reclaim some of the states the Saudis had conquered. Busy fending off the Chinese, the Saudis unwisely chose not to reclaim those African states. By the time they realized their mistake, it was too late and the New Afrikaners were on their doorstep, impolitely knocking at the gate with a force of close to four hundred thousand pissed off warriors.

Meanwhile, the United Kingdom was keeping as low a profile as possible while bulking up its borders. The very real threat of an invasion by any European nation terrified the population.

The British military, while strong in the sense of willingness to overcome overwhelming odds, was also practical. In another surprise move that second week of the chaos, the United Kingdom appealed to the United States of the Americas to let them join their federation.

The States did not need a second invitation.

The running joke among the States' citizens was this was sweet payback for the 1776 Revolutionary War and it had only taken two hundred or so years to declare the United Kingdom a Unites States territory.

In time, the United Kingdom planned to get the last laugh. Strategically, the great island was in perfect place to rule both Europe and the States. What it needed to be able to do this was more land. For centuries, England had ruled parts of the world with strong military might, but now, with heavy artillery so readily available, even the smallest nation could become a threat to its larger neighbor.

The Brits knew this from both sides: first as a smaller country that had at one time ruled the much larger continent of Australia and second as a smaller country that always had the underlying fear of conquest by a larger, aggressive European neighbor.

Hence, the United Kingdom's appeal to the States was not a sign of defeat. Rather, it was a calculated way to buy time and build up a force of military culled from disillusioned States' patriots.

While all of this was going on, neutral Switzerland was finally overrun by the French/German coalition. Against all hope, the Swiss soon realized it was only a matter of time before they would be conquered by one nation or another. The army of former accountants and office managers was no match for the trained military of France and Germany.

The Swiss tried, though. The skirmishes were quick and deadly. The Swiss Army had been spread thin throughout Switzerland, and during the battles, they had been forced backward toward the middle of the country. All too soon, the borders shrank as the Swiss Army was pressed toward the center of the nation.

The Swiss knew it was over when all of the nation's military units were within shouting distance of each other. At that point, the Swiss government conceded that any continued fighting was futile. The bulk of the army consisted of ordinary Swiss citizens, not Spartans.

Meanwhile, Australia secured its massive coastline with a combination of men and mines left over from WWII. Attention was strictly paid to the location of the mines, which were strategically placed an eighth of a mile from land. Any sea vessel attempting to land would be in for a nasty surprise.

Because of its remoteness, Australia was the least affected by the chaos. Life for the typical Australian continued pretty much the same as it always had. The populace knew what was going on between the superpowers, but until the conflict landed in their own yard, they did not give a flying flick what happened to the rest of the world.

With the border secure, Australia crossed its arms and watched as the shit hit fans across the world.

The Chaos ruled all other countries and nations in the world. Because of the advances of telecommunications, technology, and weaponry, events that might have taken weeks to happen took only days or even hours. Some smaller countries were overrun in short periods of time, with Romania holding the record at twenty-eight minutes from the time it organized its military forces to the time those same military forces laid down their arms to the Russian-controlled Ukrainian forces.

Everywhere, might and military muscle dominated the day. The strong overtook the weak and no amount of reasoning made a difference. Some people welcomed the change, especially those in already repressed countries. Some balked and rebelled, but were soon squashed like bugs. Others ran and hid; life for them became so hard the majority eventually came back to the fold of whatever power held sway over their lives.

The very few in the States who did not know the events of the chaos were in for a very rude awakening when they finally emerged from their seclusion. Most of these were hunters or campers or hikers. A few were survivalists who had purposely cut off contact with the world they hated.

And then, there were the two who had purposely secluded themselves to regroup and plan how they would fight the known and unknown enemies responsible for destroying both of their lives.

The world they knew when they had gone into hiding had changed drastically and the pair were in for a radical awakening like nothing they had experienced.

8.

As Joe loaded supplies in the back of the old pickup truck, he noticed the absence of any of Liz's gear. In fact, he had noticed Liz's enthusiasm for leaving their safe camp had diminished somewhat in the past few days, but he had attributed her reluctance to fear.

Stepping back into their cabin, he saw Liz bent over the table marking a map she had spread out. The intense look on her face did not cover the pallor Joe had commented on at the beginning of the week which Liz had brushed off as nothing. Joe had kept at her about what was wrong until she had finally told him it was a woman thing.

Joe shut up and left her alone after that. There was nothing to compare to the viciousness and brutality as a woman at that time of the month.

But, it began to worry Joe as Liz grew paler and paler. His experience with women was enough for him to know that there was something more going on than what Liz had told him.

"Where's your stuff?" Joe asked.

Liz looked up and Joe saw that in addition to her pallor, the whites of her eyes had a yellowish tinge. Startled, Joe stepped toward Liz as she sat down.

"Liz, why didn't you tell me you were sick?" Joe had seen enough in his life to know that Liz was seriously ill.

Liz rested her head on one hand and looked at Joe sidewise. With a sad smile, she told him exactly what he did not want to hear.

"I thought I'd short-circuited it after I dug the ghoul out of my arm." She sighed heavily as she continued. "I guess I didn't."

"What are you talking about?" Joe asked as he gently touched her pale face. Her clammy skin felt cool and rubbery, and Joe had to resist jerking his hand back.

She felt dead.

"Muveed puts a little something extra in field agents,"

she replied as she touched the hand resting on her face. As if she knew how Joe was feeling, she took his hand away and rested it on the table and covered it with hers.

"It's not foolproof, but for the most part, it's lethal. I don't know all the details, I just know that I've got a microscopic nano attached to my spine. We all had them implanted when we started working on the outside.

"Every nano has something different. Looks like mine was loaded with some kind of kidney cancer. It's activated if Muveed determines you're a threat or if they confirm an enemy's got you. Usually, it's a matter of hours before you're dead, but I guess I actually did short-circuit something in it that made it take longer to actually activate."

Liz sadly looked at Joe's stricken face as she continued.

"I knew it was active two weeks ago. I thought I'd killed it, but I guess I'd just bought myself a little more time."

"We could get you to a . . ." Joe started to say as Liz interrupted him.

"No hospitals, Joe. Most of the medical places have Muveed in them and they'd know right away what was happening. I'd rather die here, free, than go to a Muveed prison."

Joe was choking up as he looked at the woman who had risked her life to save his. There was nothing he could to save her; his medical knowledge was severely limited and he completely understood the risk she would take if she went to any medical facility.

Liz reached around and picked up a large folder off of the kitchen counter. When she turned back around and saw Joe's face, she slapped him and gave him a ghost of a grin.

"Don't cry, little girl," she said as she laughed quietly. "If it's any comfort, you'll probably be dead, too, before the end of the year."

Liz's face hardened as she continued. "But, take as many of them with you as you can before you go.

"Avenge me, Joe. Fuckin' avenge me."

After a few moments of silence, Liz opened the folder. "Okay, let's get started," she said as she handed Joe a stack of papers. "I've written down everything I could think of about Muveed, their operations, locations – all their shit. I know we've talked about a lot of this, but I've written down everything I could remember in case I forgot something.

"These papers," she said as she handed Joe another stack of papers, "are from Dad. He had them in a lockbox that I got to before I came to see you in Normal. Most of what's in Dad's papers is encryption codes for Muveed databases. Muveed's probably changed a lot of those codes, but there might be a few they overlooked. It won't hurt for you to try because once you get in one database at this level, you can access lower-level encrypted information."

Liz frowned as she looked at one of the papers. Joe watched as emotions played across her face.

"One more thing and it's personal: I want you to promise you'll do something for me. Tony's little brother's in school at Attamatox; they sent him to boarding school because he was messing up bad at home and embarrassing the crap out of Tony's folk. He's the closest to family I've got left. Somebody needs to know what happened to Tony and me.

"Will you do that for me, Joe?"

Joe started choking up again as he agreed to do whatever she wanted him to do. As Liz playfully raised her hand to slap him again, he smiled and caught her hand in his.

"You know," Joe told her, "You're just like your Dad. He was tough as steel, but he was always looking out for other people."

"Dad would never admit it, but he loved you guys, especially you. I told you before, he saw something in you.

"Now, here's all the info you need to find Tony's brother, Benny. I want you to tell him everything. After you tell him, I want you to get him to this safe house in Alberta. He's old enough he'll be able to make it on his own from there. I just want him out of it all."

Liz gathered all the papers and put them back in the folder. "I'm guessing I have a few days left, but you need to get out of here now. I'm worried about Benny. If Muveed gets to him first, he's lost. His parents won't help him 'cause they live and breathe Muveed."

Joe stood up. After just the short time he had spent with Liz, he knew better than to argue with her. As he gathered up the last remaining items he needed, Liz handed him the folder.

"I don't have to tell you, but I will anyway: stay off the main roads. Muveed won't give up looking for us too easily." Liz stood up and gave Joe a quick hug. "Get out of here, Joe. I'm tired and I need to rest," she said as she stretched out on the couch.

Joe covered her with a blanket and gently kissed the top of her head. As he turned to leave, Liz grabbed his hand.

"Avenge me. Avenge my father," Liz softly said as she closed her tired eyes.

Joe left the camp with a heavy heart. He owed Liz his life and he was going to repay that debt. Whether it was helping Tony's brother or taking down Muveed, someway, somehow, he would repay Liz for saving him.

The old truck rattled and creaked as he drove down the bumpy road leading away from the hunahas kanitas. Sorrow for Liz was turning into vengeance and he filed this feeling away in a compartment in his mind with the others.

Beanie, Sarge, and now, Liz. His thirst for justice for those lost lives, and his own lost life, was unending. Over the past year, his emotions had gone from fear and confusion to realization and, finally, lethal hatred.

As Joe traveled that first day, his thoughts were on finding and killing all those involved in the deaths of those close to him. Because he was concentrating so deeply on his own thoughts, he almost missed the first telltale sign that something was not right with his country.

Along the road, he noticed an abundance of military vehicles. Before he knew it, he was trapped in traffic heading into Meader, Nebraska, with a military road block up ahead and soldiers standing on alert along the side of the road. With a sick feeling in his stomach, Joe was forced to creep along the road with the other cars toward the checkpoint.

When Joe pulled up to the roadblock, he did not know if he would be able to talk his way out of the dangerous situation. He knew he would not be able to use firepower; he was seriously outnumbered by the soldiers. His only chance would be using his wits.

Unfortunately, his wits weren't what they used to be.

"License, sir," the guard demanded.

As Joe fumbled for his wallet, the guard impatiently tapped the side of the truck.

"Sir, you are required to display your Liberty License badge in your vehicle window at all times."

Motioning a soldier to Joe's truck, the guard continued as the soldier raised his weapon and pointed it directly at Joe's head. "Pull over to the side, sir, and exit your vehicle."

Joe's stomach dropped as he eased his vehicle over. He was hemmed in on all sides, by either military vehicles or town traffic. Add to the fact that there must be fifty or sixty armed soldiers along the road, and one with his weapon trained on Joe's head, and Joe's passing thoughts of flight were just that – passing.

Joe got out of the truck with his hands raised. As the soldier held him at gunpoint, another soldier frisked Joe. The soldier found his wallet, opened it, took out his driver's license, and handed it to an officer who had walked over. As the soldier continued to pat Joe down, he found the .22 Joe had tucked in his boot.

Joe thought that was the end.

"Sir, this is invalid," the officer said as he held Joe's driver's license. "Where is your Liberty License, sir?"

Honesty at this point seemed to be the best policy for Joe. "I don't know what a Liberty License is. What's going on here?"

"Sir, are you a citizen of the United States of the Americas?"

"The United States of the what?" Joe asked.

"Of the Americas, sir." The officer looked at Joe a little closer and seemed to realize something. "Sir, where have you just come from?"

Joe also had a realization at that moment. Whatever had gone down in the past month was bigger than big, but the hunt for Joe was not at the center of it.

Relaxing slightly, Joe replied, "Lieutenant, I just got back from a three-week retreat at a camp in Sedio, North Dakota." Looking around, Joe asked, "Can you tell me what the hell is going on?"

The officer nodded to the soldiers surrounding them and the weapon pointed at Joe's head was lowered.

"Sir, come with me," the officer said as the guard handed Joe back his gun.

If ever Joe felt like he had stepped out of real life and into the rabbit hole, it was at that moment.

As Joe and the lieutenant walked toward the guardhouse by the roadblock, the officer began to tell Joe of the changes in the country and the world that had taken place during the short time Joe had been out of touch.

Luckily, the lieutenant did not probe too deeply into why Joe had been out of touch. Joe's license had not started bells and alarms, so he was not being drilled about anything in his recent past.

Rather, the lieutenant offered Joe coffee as they sat at the table inside the guardhouse as he explained to Joe in condensed detail what had happened around the world within the past few weeks.

Joe was stunned, but not surprised. The icy feeling in his veins came from the knowledge that he was at least partially responsible for the chaos. Nations had run unchecked; the referee for the superpowers lost the ability to interpret the scorebook.

The keys locked inside Joe's head were the only things that would have stopped the world from spiraling down the cataclysmic drain. Now, it seemed the world was headed for the Last War as definitive lines were drawn.

Joe learned that travel was restricted outside the new United States of the Americas except for military personnel. That blew any plans he had made to sneak over to Europe and set things deadly with the Presatical.

As everything sunk in, Joe asked, "What happened to U. S. citizens abroad?"

"We were able to bring as many as possible home, sir. The embassies were evacuated at the first sign of the Chaos and all troops stationed abroad were recalled to home base. Foreign nationals were expelled from U. S. territory and our borders secured."

The lieutenant took a piece of paper out of a cubbyhole and wrote something on it before handing it to Joe.

"This is a pass you'll need to give the Citizen Identity Department in town, sir. They'll see to it you get your citizen's license and you won't have to go through this again."

Looking hard at Joe as they left the guardhouse, the lieutenant told Joe, "Make sure you get this done today, sir. We wouldn't want you to end up in a work camp."

Joe caught the drift. He had to get this new identity to prove his citizenship or it was off to the new United States gulag.

As Joe drove away from the roadblock and into town, he watched in his rearview mirror for any telltale sign that the lieutenant was contacting people Joe would not want contacted. It looked like Joe was in the clear, though, as he watched the lieutenant walk toward a group of cars and not to the post phone inside the guardhouse.

Intuitively, Joe had given the soldier his real driver's license and not the fake one he and Liz had concocted. He gave the real one with his real name not knowing if it would cause him to end up in jail or back with Muveed – he still did not know why he had taken the risk, but his intuition proved to be right. At least this way, he would not have to pretend to be someone he was not.

While this put a kink in any plans Joe had made, it might work to his advantage. Muveed was just as trapped here in the States as he was, and this would make finding them much easier.

With the borders closed, everyone would be under a close watch by the military and by local law enforcement.

Joe did not think he would have much of a problem once he got his new identity card.

Out of all the things the lieutenant had told him, he never would have thought it would become mandatory for U. S. citizens to carry firearms. Except in Texas, of course.

And that was another thing: if someone had told him a month ago the center of federal government would be moved from the District of Columbia to Texas, he would have laughed and called that person a liar to their face.

As Joe stepped into the Citizens Identity Office, he wondered what else in his world had changed.

.

9.

Business was slow.

Interesting, adrenaline-pumping business was deader than a belly-up armadillo by the side of the road. The regular boring business of death was still the same. People still died of disease and from car accidents, but violent deaths from violent means were way down.

The morgue was a dull place to be nowadays.

If there was one thing the good coroner knew very well, it was boredom. His time spent as head of the Coroner's Department and chief flunky in the morgue had been, save for a few exciting spots, excessively boring.

Drinking helped. Besides numbing him from the daily monotony of his work, drinking made him forget everything else. Vatamo vodka was his medicine of choice and he always kept a few bottles in the bottom of an unused corpse locker.

The rest of the crew were fully aware of Dr. Ian Tanaki's secret stash. Secret was not quite the word to use since he did nothing to hide his preferred addiction. Politely hidden was more apt.

Dr. Tanaki's two top assistants knew better than to touch the bottles, at least, for most of the time. The good doctor could detect even the slightest movement of his precious bottles. Sometimes, when things got too tediously boring, Goza and Hank would move a bottle or two half a centimeter one way or another, and sit back and watch Dr. Tanaki have a mini fit.

No matter how much he drank, the doctor's powers of observation were astounding. It had always been that way and this damned ability had hurt him more than it had helped.

Drinking did not help the doctor slide down the hole to the abyss of oblivion. Tying a good one on was not much of an option these days. Dr. Tanaki had developed a high tolerance for alcohol over the years. Guzzling a fifth of

Vatamo vodka just gave him severe heartburn and a bad case of the runs.

The last time something had pulled him up out of his self-imposed debauchery, it had hit way too close to his past. A woman killed by her husband was not entirely new, but a police officer killing his own wife was a bit out of the ordinary.

That death and the crime scene still haunted him despite his attempts to erase the memory with liquor. Not that he was not used to gruesome crimes; he had witnessed enough in his career.

But this one was very different. The kitchen had shown signs of a very brutal struggle; blood was pooling in different areas and arterial spray had laced the ceiling with eerie rust-red stripes.

The suspect, a local police officer Dr. Tanaki knew and liked, was sitting calmly on a barstool while the victim lay in a lake of blood on the floor a few yards from him. When Dr. Tankaki bent down to examine the fatal wound, he saw something at the hairline of the victim that made his heart stop.

What could have passed for a tiny, irregular scar with any other medical personnel sent Dr. Tanaki scurrying out of the cop's house in a panic. It had been twenty-nine years since he had seen the sign of the kagi.

The last time he had seen the deliberate emblem of a key on a human body had been when he was a different man in a different land. At that time, he had been known as Dr. Miko Lee and he had been a pawn to the most powerful man in the world.

At that time, so many years ago, he had been the assistant to the physician / psychiatrist who was responsible for stirring the minds of simpletons like one would stir scrambled eggs.

Whether it succeeded or not, each sad experiment had been marked with the sign of the kagi. The markings were like a sick, medical brand. These brands meant that subject's mind or body, or both, had been tampered with in ways no human's body should be made to bear.

The kagi branding extended to other poor souls as well. Those who were in service to the ruler of the world also bore the kagi mark.

Dr. Tanaki's nightmares about that time in his life were heavy with the loss of his family. After his mentor died, he had been earmarked to take his place and continue his abominable work.

If he had accepted this position, he would have been no better than the horrid Nazi doctors of World War II who subjected innocent humans to inhuman experiments. He would have become inhuman, himself, just as his mentor who, after years of tampering with bodies and minds, had become a soulless man.

If he had turned down the chance to step into his mentor's shoes, he and his family would have died, but not before his wife and children had been tortured in front of him. His captors would have wanted all the information he carried in his mind and this method of extraction always succeeded – he knew first hand, since he had seen this form of persuasion used on others.

The good doctor ran. He left his home, his country, and his family. He had no idea what had happened to his wife and children, but he knew they would not have been allowed to live, not after his defection.

He prayed daily they were given merciful deaths.

Then, twenty-nine years later, Dr. Tanaki's past caught up with him. He had always hoped against hope that the diabolical men and women he had left behind had died or drifted apart.

It was a shock that took almost a year for the doctor to recover from. He barely drank during the past months, but he also hadn't slept. Thankfully, his work did not suffer and none of his patients in the morgue ever complained.

The new world was not that new to Dr. Tanaki. Over the course of his life, he had seen country after country gain power and lose power. It was an endless game powerful men played all the time with which he was all too familiar.

Recently, with the shift in power to central Texas, Dr. Tanaki had been conscripted to serve several days a month as physician to living, breathing soldiers. The last time, he had been assigned a strange company of silent men who completely unnerved him with their fish-dead eyes.

One in particular, quite a bit older than the rest, had watched his every move and when Dr. Tanaki started his physical, this one had spoken to him in the Imperial language.

Jumping slightly, Dr. Tanaki pretended not to have heard him. The soldier repeated himself and Dr. Tanaki again acted as if he did not understand. When the doctor did not respond, the soldier grabbed his arm and pushed Dr. Tanaki's sleeve up.

The sign of the kagi was also branded on those who served. Dr. Miko Li had sliced the brand off his forearm before he became Dr. Ian Tanaki and all that was left was a faded scar.

The soldier dropped the doctor's arm and spoke one last time, this time in English.

"We'll be waiting for you, Miko," he said before he and his company left the clinic.

He was too tired to run anymore. He was too old to run anymore. He just wanted to be with his family in whatever heaven they were living.

After that first initial shock, resignation set in and with every knock at the door, Miko expected to be hogtied and dragged out of the morgue.

What happened was not that far from what he expected.

A small group of men found him nine days after the episode at the military clinic. When they came in, he knew there was no hope for him. He did not resist when they tied his hands. He was passive when they injected him with what he hoped was a lethal dose of anything, but turned out to be a sedative.

He did not put up a fuss when they stripped his clothes off and put a hospital gown on him. He still did not object when the dead-eyed men lifted him on one of the steel autopsy tables.

He felt a scream building in him when his fuzzy mind comprehended that thick, black body bag he was being stuffed into. Had he not been sedated, he would have lost his mind as the darkness closed upon him.

The last thing he saw was the silver zipper as it was closed above his head.

Meanwhile, his unfortunate assistants had come back early from lunch and were now resting eternally behind their desks with heads bent at awkward angles. Their bloodless deaths were small consolations to their loved ones.

The police investigating the deaths and the disappearance of the coroner came to the conclusion that the good doctor, who was known as a total lush, had finally snapped. Their guess was he had lost his mind and killed his assistants, then taken off for parts unknown.

In reality, Miko was now an unwilling resident in the town of Normal. Although the Muveed and the Presatical at times collaborated, this was not one of those times. For the past three years, Vincent Tumin had known where Miko was in a general way, but had been unable to pinpoint the doctor's exact location.

Up until three weeks before, that is. An American soldier, who was also Muveed, had spotted Miko. After that, it was only a matter of time before Vincent gave the word to seize and secure the doctor.

Miko groggily came to his senses. As he became more and more aware of the brightness of his surroundings, he began to realize he was in a clinical setting. When his eyes finally cleared, he was able to see a man sitting in the corner.

As he turned his head to the left to better see the man, the small amount of spit in his mouth dried up instantly. Miko's heart started racing and his bladder lost all its discipline.

"Welcome back, Miko," Vincent said. "We have a lot of catching up to do."

With those words, Miko's world was no longer his own.

10.

Joe felt more and more like Alice in Wonderland as the day passed.

When he walked into the Citizens' Identity Office, his first thought was he had walked into Utopia. When the caseworker assigned to him asked him to roll up his sleeves, Joe just looked at him.

"Identifying marks, sir," the office jockey said. "If you've been in the service, you're granted carte blanche privileges within the scope of the new laws."

Rolling up his sleeves, the worker looked at Joe's military tattoos and smiled as he nodded.

"I could tell by your bearing, sir, that you were either army or marine," he said as he filled out the paperwork for Joe's new identity card. "I'll have you out of here in just a few minutes, sir.

"If you'd like to register your firearms now, I could expedite that for you, too." The worker looked sharply at Joe as he continued. "You do pack, don't you, sir?"

Joe laughed as he told the desk jockey, "Hell, yeah."

As the worker relaxed, Joe again wondered what rabbit hole he had dropped into. People required to carry firearms, military given prestige above non-military, and Texas the capital of the country.

Well, whatever psycho civilization he had wandered into, he liked it.

"Sir, this is your new identity card. If you lose it, you'll be issued a new one and the old one will deactivate. All of your information is stored on a chip inside the card and in our database. As military, you already have five thousand credits, which equals roughly a dollar per credit."

Holding up the Joe's new identity card, the worker continued. "As a citizen of the new United States of the Americas, you swear to uphold the laws of the military and of the government. You swear to be vigilant and to protect yourself and other citizens against those outside of our nation. You swear to be vigilant and to protect your fellow citizens should the need arise."

The worker looked at Joe and waited. Joe looked back at him.

"You're supposed to agree, sir," the worker said.

"Oh," Joe replied. "I agree to everything."

"Thank you, sir. Now, if you'd just sign your full name, Mr. Daniels, you can be on your way."

Joe signed the papers, pocketed his new identity card, took back his guns, and left.

In the open air, he was waiting for someone to come after him. Of all the things he had imagined might be going on in the world while he was in seclusion, this was not one of them.

The world was not as it seemed. The world he thought he had known was radically different. Climbing into his truck, he realized the tattoos he wore carried more weight in this new country than anything in his pockets.

A month ago when he had gone with Liz into the survivalists' camp, the United States had been a country pandering to too many special interests, too many foreign countries, and too many lost causes.

The country he had stepped back into was a far cry from the namby-pamby one he had known. It was now the United we'll-kick-your-ass States of the Americas.

Joe wondered how the Muveed were surviving in the new regime. Knowing what he knew about them, this was keeping in line with their beliefs. Since a large majority of the Muveed were military, it was scary to think how the new laws fit hand in hand with the unspoken laws of the Muveed.

That got Joe to wondering: were the Muveed the power behind the new United States? It did not seem possible that they would have access to everything that it took to move a country from passivity to aggression.

But, Joe had been wrong before, so this scenario was entirely possible. Just like the scenarios of Tony, Liz, Sarge, Beanie – they were all connected in a bizarre and twisted fashion.

Could all of the chaos and changes simply be the spiral downspin from the impotency of the Presatical? Without the keys, supposedly, he could not control the countries he was responsible for controlling.

It was a daunting question.

A part of Joe felt hugely responsible for the mess in which the world had gotten itself. Another part of him felt guilt over the hurt and death that had happened because of him. A big part of him was just pissed.

The town of Meader, Nebraska, felt weird. Not really the town itself, but the people in the town. Citizens were coming and going, and no one was loitering. Everyone seemed to be moving around with a purpose.

It was not typical behavior for a medium sized town like this one. As he drove down the main street, he never once saw a crowd of freeloaders hanging around the outside of stores, doing nothing.

Pulling into a convenience store, Joe came out with a six-pack, four newspapers, and three magazines. Although he did not fully trust the media to tell the whole truth and nothing but the truth, he figured he would get a better angle on what the fuck had happened in his absence from print than from rumors and gossip.

More than anything, though, he needed the beer.

Finding a parking space in front of a well-kept duck pond in front of a large hotel, Joe stopped his truck, grabbed the beer and papers, and parked himself on a bench. The ducks waddled over to him looking for a handout.

"All I've got is beer, buddies," Joe told the noisy crowd.

Realizing Joe was a lost cause, the duck troop marched back into the water. Joe watched the ducks and jumped a little when a hand tapped him on his shoulder.

"ID, please," a stone-faced police officer requested. Joe had not heard a vehicle and had been totally unaware that someone had crept up behind him. He did not want to think he was losing his sense of detection, but something was off-kilter.

Joe handed the police officer his newly minted identity

card. As soon as the officer looked at it, he relaxed and handed it back to Joe.

"Sorry about that, Mr. Daniels," he said. "Not too many people come down to the pond in the middle of the day and management called to report a suspicious character."

He paused and said, "Excuse me for a minute while I call this in."

Getting on his radio, Joe heard him telling the manager at the hotel that all was well.

"Sorry, again," Officer Haney told Joe. "You've registered your weapon, haven't you? If not, I could take care of that for you."

Joe was a bit baffled. At this point in the strange alternate reality world he had been dropped in, he was not hesitant to ask why he was getting special treatment.

"Your identity card is green-lighted. The worker should have explained that to you."

"He told me I had carte blanche, whatever that means," Joe replied.

"Mr. Daniels, except for military government officials, you have equal privileges alongside officers such as myself and other military personnel."

The officer sat on the bench with Joe and continued. "The best thing I can do for you is get you in one of our orientation classes. There aren't too many in these classes, but we have occasional stragglers like yourself," he said with a laugh.

"Thanks," Joe replied. "Is it okay if I stay here for awhile?" he asked as he waved his hand toward the beer and papers. "I was trying to catch up."

The officer laughed again. "Sure thing. The hotel knows who you are now, so don't worry about them." He held out his hand as he got up. "It's a pleasure to meet you, sir." He smiled as he handed Joe his card. "If you need a ride after that six-pack, call one of us to pick you up."

Joe watched the officer leave and then turned back to his beer and papers. The headlines screamed at him about coalitions dissolved, power nations gobbling up weaker ones, and neighboring countries at each other's throats.

The situation in the States was different. People were different. The average citizen seemed to have become a gun-toting, law-enforcing army of one and a collective of many. To Joe, it felt uneasily like military communism.

Inside the front section of each paper, Joe saw the same short list of criminal offenses and their consequences. There were no longer differentiations between the same crimes: physical offenses were all lumped under physical assault, property damages in all forms were classified as property assault, burglary was burglary, and murder was murder.

Shooting someone who committed any of these crimes was not only acceptable, but encouraged under the "Good Citizen's Act." This new law gave immunity to anyone who saved the courts time by taking the law into their own hands. It had been passed in the new seat of government in Texas, of course.

There were guidelines to which citizens had to adhere. Guilt for any of the four crimes had to be witnessed, documented, and called or text messaged to a new special division in the police department called the Citizen Enforcement Unit, or CEU, or the ever-popular "See You." To keep citizens from abusing the new system, there had to be at least two additional witnesses to the crime.

Most citizens had CEU on speed dial on their cell phones. CEU provided text messaging templates to speed up the process and all calls, text messages, and picture images were free to send. Wireless providers were in agony as profits dropped when these free government services outweighed paid services ninety to one.

Strongly worded warnings were placed alongside the list of crimes and the crime control guidelines. Personal vendettas against otherwise innocent citizens would not be tolerated. False accusations were punishable by life in a prison work camp or quick execution.

Joe kept reading and slowly drew a picture of the upside-down society he had landed in. Vigilantism was the rule of the day. As he read between the lines, he began to draw a clearer understanding of what now was considered normal in the new United States.

Odd pockets of resistance were still around, the papers stated. In the National Digest, some of the rebels against the new society and its laws fought day and night to keep their former ways of life.

Strangely, the rebels one would think would revolt against the new society seemed to embrace it. Motorcycle gangs, once the ultimate symbol of man against authority, were now legal thugs, strict adherents to and enforcers of the new laws.

City gangs surprised everyone. Their new strict codes of honor and loyalty transferred to the new military keepers of the States with hardly a blip. Because the gangs were disciplined within their own cliques, it was easy to assimilate them into the military.

One of the major deciding factors for both the bikers and the gangs was the real threat of lethal vigilantism from millions of gun-toting, CEUs. They outnumbered the bad boys five hundred to one.

Joe continued to flip through the papers and became intrigued by the normal news past the front page. Gas prices were rising, again, and the killer heat in the Midwest had affected wheat crops, which in turn had affected food prices.

In the entertainment section, the exploits of Joe's favorite hard-core metal band, Fusion, showed they had not slowed down because the world changed. Rather, their behavior was embraced (or excused) by the new country because of their past and present extreme patriotism.

Sports remained sports. Wrestling was still one of the highest watched shows on cable, along with reality shows. Race season was right around the corner and the bad boys of the racetrack had upped the ante of outrageous conduct.

The baseball strike was still in full swing, no pun intended. Joe's favorite team, the Kicks, had been having a good run before the strike. His second favorite, the Rocks, had been trying to climb out of the worst season in their history.

On the political page, the President heartily embraced each new law the new military government put into effect. Joe realized he had no choice, since to go against the new country's enforcers would be mean an end to his public office. Since the president had been lukewarm on the military during his term, his endorsement for the new laws was amusing.

No mention of foreign aid. All that was written in regard to countries outside the United States of the Americas was sketchy at best. For all intents and purposes, the world outside the States did not exist.

The new America had closed its borders with a resounding slam.

The sun was going down and Joe's beer had gotten warm. He had been so engrossed in what he had been reading that he hadn't been aware the day had slipped away. It was too late to go to the library to dig up anything he could on current events relating to the Muveed or the Presatical.

Given what he had been reading, those secret societies could not be faring too well, particularly the Muveed members who were still in the States. With all the documentation needed now, and the current feeling of distrust of anything foreign, Vincent and his henchmen had probably skipped the country while they still could.

Joe thought about finding an internet café to do a little more digging, but he felt uncomfortable using a computer in this new society. He had no idea who might be looking over his shoulder and until he could get a personal laptop, he was not willing to chance being found out.

Joe stood up and noticed for the first time the couple who were sitting on the opposite side of the pond. The girl was holding the boy's hand and the boy had his arm around the girl's shoulder.

The boy was packing heat in a holster slung across his chest and from what Joe could tell from the distance, the girl's pink plaid purse had a ready-made holster on the side.

When he stood up, they both glanced toward him and

then went back to talking and cuddling. It was sweet and surreal, a mix of young love and Wild West gun slinging.

Gathering his papers, Joe walked toward his truck. After putting the papers on the seat beside him, he set for a few moments relishing the peace and quiet. Before he could start the engine, he heard a strange yelp.

Jerking his head in the direction of the sound, he saw the boy down on the ground and the girl being held from behind by a large man. Two other thugs were beating the boy and even from where Joe was sitting, he could see blood spraying into the air.

On auto-pilot, Joe leapt from the truck with his .32 in hand as he raced around the perimeter of the pond. Ducking low, he quickly surveyed his odds against three large thugs with what looked like AK's.

Why they hadn't fired already was obvious. They were vicious, but not stupid. As soon as they would open up, the police would be called along with whatever CEUs were in the vicinity.

Creeping silently behind bushes, Joe came within twenty feet of the scene. In and out, pop and split – his military and mercenary training had automatically kicked in.

Taking quick aim at one of the thugs as he stood up, Joe fired and made his mark. Thug number one dropped as the left side of his head dissolved.

The roar of the gun was sure to bring out someone to help, but not soon enough to save what was left of the boy on the ground. Aiming again within two seconds of dropping the first thug, Joe's second target had slipped into a crouching position.

If the thug thought making himself a smaller target would help, he was lethally mistaken. Joe simply shot him twice, double-tapping chest and head, before he could raise his AK.

Joe slipped like a ghost to another bush ten feet away. Two down and one to go, but this one was holding the girl in front of him like a shield.

As Joe watched, the girl started doing some kind of

crazy backwards dance with her feet. Building momentum, the girl was able to push hard enough to topple both herself and the thug. As they fell to the ground, the girl rolled away and out of reach.

Joe took the opportunity to put an end to thug number three.

Coming into the open with one hand holding his gun and the other held out, Joe kicked the guns away from dead hands, just in case one of them had survived. It was not likely, especially for the guy with half a head, but Joe was not taking any chances.

The girl was crying as she bent over the boy. Although he was still alive, he did not look too good. Looking up at Joe, the girl simply said, "Please help me."

Luckily, the three gunshots had attracted hotel employees and Joe could hear sirens in the distance. To be on the safe side since he was quickly being outnumbered by citizens with guns, he laid his gun to the side and was putting his hands behind his head in surrender.

"NO," the girl said as Joe dropped to his knees.

Looking at the crowd gathering and unholstering their own guns, the girl addressed the crowd: "He saved us. He killed those bastards," she said as she took Joe's hand and drew him to his feet.

One of the people in the crowd closest to Joe picked up Joe's gun and handed it back to him. With that gesture, Joe started thinking that maybe this new set of standards for his country was not so bad after all.

The police and ambulance arrived at the same time. The girl, whose name was Larisa, told the police everything that had happened as quickly as she could. Anxiously, Larisa wanted to go with her boyfriend as he was being lifted into the ambulance.

Before she ran to jump in ambulance, she turned and hugged Joe. The lights from the police car and ambulance masked the flash bulb of a camera in the crowd.

Joe was "invited" back to the police station to give a more in-depth statement. At the station, instead being interrogated like he thought he would be, Joe was treated like a hero. A brief questioning and a cup of coffee later, and Joe was free to go.

In a bizarre turn of events, as Joe was leaving the station, several police officers who were just coming off their shift invited Joe for drinks at a local bar.

Of course, Joe accepted. If anyone had told him the day before that he would have stepped into this alternate reality world of the new States, shot and killed three people, and then had celebratory drinks with a few of the town's policemen, he would have told them they were full of shit.

11.

The edges were disintegrating because the center could not hold.

The thought repeated itself in Vincent's mind as he sat at his desk. The compound in Normal was showing signs that all was not well. The first indication had come the day before when four of the men closest to him simply disappeared.

No one had seen them go, or else, no one was talking. A heavy sense of doom hung low over the Muveed town. The silence when he walked among his people was one of uneasiness, not the silence of respect that he was used to.

Vincent tapped a pencil against his desk. The rhythmic sound calmed him a little, but his stress level was the highest it had ever been. He had faced so many roadblocks and setbacks and dangers during his tenure as the leader of Muveed, but this new challenge was different in ways he had never encountered or imagined.

Countries had come and gone; alliances had formed and dissolved, but they'd never fallen completely apart and isolated themselves to such a great degree. The world had split into five distinct and warmongering divisions and Vincent was stuck in the most powerful of them all.

His communications with the European sector had been sporadic and disturbing. As far as he could decipher, the overseas group had been forcibly dissolved with many casualties during the French-Germanic invasion of Switzerland.

All that was left to Vincent was an impending sense of dissolution. Even the capture of Dr. Miko Li had been tainted with the knowledge that the secrets locked inside the good doctor were useless to Vincent.

Useless, because the Presatical had been destroyed and the keepers of the keys had vanished. When Vincent heard the news, he had been torn between glee and sorrow, for his one-time adversary had also been his reluctant partner in keeping the world in line.

From what he could put together, the end had come quickly and without fuss. The Presatical had been in his "secret" fortress – which had apparently not been too secret – and met his end without cowardice or bravery.

He had simply died by the hand of his second on orders from the coalition before it had fallen completely apart.

In keeping with the olden times, his head had been displayed outside the gates of the fortress in which he had been hiding. Life over the past few months had obviously not been kind to the man. According to Vincent's last remaining sources, his face was drawn and looked like that of a man much, much older.

A last ditch effort was made to find the savants. After the Presatical had ordered them taken to a safe place, they had been moved again without the second's knowledge. This did not come to light until after the Presatical was dead and the second had vanished.

After that, all of the information Vincent had accumulated dried up. His communications came to a dead stop. Now, the only way he could find anything out was through the worthless papers this upstart new country called news.

Internet between countries had been cut off, and in some places, it was entirely gone. Unauthorized wireless communication between the States and any country outside of the new union was considered a treasonable act.

In some of the more remote European countries, time had reverted back to the Dark Ages. Basic life was reduced to Third World conditions. Powers toppled quickly in these countries and were gobbled up by their neighbors. Unfortunately, a change in leadership did nothing to help the people, who were still beyond destitute.

That was all the news Vincent had. Nothing had come out of Europe for a week and he feared the last of the European Muveed were gone or had been absorbed into whatever country they'd been in at the time of society's collapse.

For the first time in his life, he was at an impasse. He did not know which way to go. His indecision was increased by the desertion of those four who had been inside Vincent's inner circle.

The last decisions he had made had been at the beginning of everything coming apart. He had sent some of his key men, including one of the four who had deserted him, into the military to infiltrate and learn what they could.

Dr. Miko Li had been the prize for this expedition. Unfortunately, his worth had plummeted once Vincent realized Europe was off-limits to anyone in the States. His grand plan to take the savants and unlock their minds with the coerced help of Dr. Li had ended with the inaccessibility of Europe.

The Muveed in Normal were waiting for him to decide what they were to do in the new United States of the Americas. Their uneasiness mimicked Vincent's own.

A knock on his door startled him. Recovering quickly before the door opened, he was not surprised when his secretary handed him a sheet of paper with the latest population count. Seven Muveeds were unaccounted for as of the previous night, three additional had slipped away that very morning.

As his secretary left, Vincent thought how the center was dissolving quicker than he had anticipated.

Unlocking a side drawer, Vincent removed a safety box and set it on top of his desk. With a quick flick of the tumble-lock, he opened the box. The only thing inside was a passport, an identity card, and a key.

He already had his escape planned. Up through Western Canada into Alaska, a short boat ride across the Bering Strait, and into Siberia. From northern Russia, he could easily slip into any part of Europe he chose.

Well, maybe not so easily now, but, it would be better than where he was now. Every minute that passed was another minute closer to detection by the authorities in the new United States of the Americas. Very little remained secret in the new day and age, and secrecy was the modus operandi of Muveed.

Vincent tucked the three items from the safety box into his chest pocket and made sure he had a full clip in his modified glock. As he walked out of his office, he did not look back.

He chose a random car from the company garage. As he drove away, he put the town of Normal out of his mind. At the perimeter, he was stopped by one his guards. He shot him dead, and then drove away.

Back in Normal, Miko Li waited for the torture to begin. He had almost given up hope of escape. The men guarding him were silent and cold. Although he did not try to engage them in conversation, his simple requests for things like pen and paper were met with icy stares.

With each day that passed, Miko realized he would not be killed quickly. His death would be long and tortuous. He would easily give up his secrets, for he was not a brave man anymore. He knew that just a whiff of pain was enough to make him blurt out things better left hidden.

What he did not understand was why Vincent Tumin had not questioned him on this day of days. Even in his isolated room, Miko was aware of a strange undercurrent going through the people around him. It was as if the end of the world was upon them and their gloom was transparent despite their attempt to remain stoic.

His guards had drifted off. Usually, one or two were in the room with him, but on this strange day, none had shown.

Afraid of a trick, Miko had been leery of trying the door to see if it was still locked. After awhile, however, curiosity over his lack of visitors got the better of him and he cautiously attempted to open the door.

It was locked.

Miko was disappointed, but not surprised. Even though he was no longer being closely guarded, why would he be allowed to leave? It was simply wishful thinking.

Over the course of the day, no one came in. By evening, he was wondering if he had been forgotten when one of the nurses came in with a wild look in her eyes.

Instantly afraid, Miko stiffened in anticipation of violence. Instead, the nurse grabbed his hand and led him out of his room.

"Vincent is gone," she said with a shaky tremor in her voice. "No one knows where and he shot a guard on his way out of town."

Panting slightly and still holding Miko's hand, she continued.

"Half of Normal is gone. I don't know what's happened to them, but I'm leaving, too." She turned to look at Miko. "I didn't forget about you or the others. I just had to wait until it was safe."

"What others?" Miko asked.

"The ones like you, the ones Vincent brought in," she replied. "I got the ones I knew about. They're waiting for us in the basement garage."

When they reached the garage a minute later, a small group was huddled beside a van. Miko recognized two of the nurses who had attended him, but he did not recognize any of the others; the only thing he had in common with the other freed prisoners was their confusion and fear.

Everyone was hustled into the van. As they pulled away, Miko kept waiting for guards to jump out with machine guns firing bullets through the thin metal protecting him.

The streets of Normal were deserted except for a few other cars headed out of town. This was the first time Miko had seen outside of the windowless room he had been kept in and even he felt the eerie undertones of the unnaturally quiet town.

No one stopped them as they drove out of Normal.

Three hours later, they reached Wichita and the group disbanded. After a long night on a bus bound for home, Miko finally reached his house. Walking into his darkened living room, Miko felt a stirring of uneasiness as he thought he glimpsed a shadow in the corner.

His eyes had tricked him. There were no assassins waiting him and no crazy Muveeds. Nevertheless, Miko packed a quick bag and left. He would never return to the small cottage he had lived in for the last fifteen years.

Luckily, he was familiar with packing light. The last time he had left his home, it had only been with the clothes he wore. He had come to his adopted country with nothing, so he had no problem leaving his home with only a small bag.

Traveling light, Miko headed east toward the new center of government. He felt he would be safest within protective federal arms. Not only that, but he felt the closer he was to the military, the better off he would be. Muveed and the real military did not mix.

Nine hours later, Miko crossed the Texas border.

As he drove into Dallas, he was calmed and reassured by the vast military forces present. Showing his citizen's identity card and coroner's badge, Miko was waved through all checkpoints.

Once he arrived at the Dallas coroner's office, he introduced himself and told the director exactly what had happened to him and where he could find Muveed's secret city.

Miko knew the director thought he had lost his mind, but he would duty-bound to check out his story. His story was confirmed within two hours. Miko loved how quickly everything happened in this new society.

That evening in his hotel room, Miko was astonished at everything that had happened to him within the past twenty-four hours. He had been released from his prison, left his home, traveled to Dallas, told his story, had someone believe his story, been offered a job at the coroner's office, and was given an advance to tide him over until his first paycheck.

Not far away from Miko, another man from his past had been offered the opportunity to serve his country. Joe Daniels felt as though he had come full circle.

The military past he had left long ago was now his life. Enlisting in the new military, Joe felt oddly at home among the other men. In the back of his mind, he felt he had never really left.

The New Military mimicked the new United States of

the Americas. There were no divisions in military; the Army, Navy, Marines, and Air Force were all one. The New Military was now equal in all departments; in an uneasy way, it was vaguely communist in its new organization.

Endless drills and exercises prepared Joe and his squad for their eventual deployment to the border. In the new military, there were three main divisions: homeland enforcement brigades, border security companies, and overseas battalions.

Joe was not given a choice since all new recruits, whether they had served before or not, deployed first to the borders. Joe heard others talk about how little action was on the border, but he understood why newbies were first sent there.

In situations calling for quick decisiveness, such as citizen protection and battle judgments, a seasoned soldier would be the best man or woman to handle whatever came up. Even though Joe had prior experience, in the United States of the Americas military, all newbies started out on an equal footing.

This was because the original United States had conquered so many of the smaller nations in the Americas, the only way to weed out the undesirables was to place them on a front line. And the only secure front line the military could control on home ground was the border.

It did not take Joe long to figure this out.

Aside from joining, or, rejoining the military, Joe was gaining local fame as the new citizen who had saved a couple from certain death at the hands of a trio of dissidents. Larissa Nobles told anyone and everyone how Joe had come to her and her boyfriend Alex Lincoln's rescue.

Joe was not too happy with all the attention, but to say too much about it would draw even more attention to himself. The best he could do was hope something else would take its place and he could fade into the background.

No such luck. It had somehow followed him to Dallas.

Joe had decided to come to Dallas because he wanted to be closer to the center of the new government. He felt safer than he had felt in a long time because this new regime was military and he was comfortable with military.

Another reason he came was because he felt the Muveed or the Presatical or some other unknown entity had had a hand in removing any records relating to Joe after Beanie's accident. The reason he thought this was because the police department in Meader had run a routine background check on him and nothing unusual had come up.

What Joe did not know was there was no longer a Muveed or a Presatical with which he had to contend. His concern about recapture was, at the moment, unfounded, but he was unaware of his good fortune.

Joe felt Muveed would do anything and everything to get hold of him again. When he had his first military physical the week before, he had asked the doctor about his broken jaw and ribs. The physician took x-rays and showed them to Joe.

Pointing to his rib on the x-ray screen, the doctor said, "These are old. You can tell by the uneven bone growth where they healed."

Pulling another x-ray from the packet, the doctor continued, "This is your jaw. There was no facture here." He put the x-rays away. "Whoever told you that you had a broken jaw was either lying or a quack."

To Joe, this was just another mystery in his life of mysteries. The only reason he could think of for Muveed wanting him to believe he had been so badly injured was they wanted to put themselves in the "savior" mode. If they had convinced Joe he had been saved and healed by Muveed, then, in their minds, he would have been more willing to help them when the time came.

What a crock of shit. Of course, this was simply supposition on Joe's part, since there was no one from Muveed to ask.

After his physical, Joe was declared fit and ready for duty. Listening to the other recruits in his unit, he gathered that a few of them were from a local gang. Two months ago, this would have been a scene straight out of a movie.

Before his unit deployed to the border, they were all given a few days of leave. Joe spent his free time trying to contact his old computer buddy, Todd.

Todd was MIA. At a computer in the local library, Joe scoured hundreds of blogs that Todd might have been on, but found nothing. Todd had once said he could go so deep underground, gophers wouldn't be able to find him.

Apparently, Todd had done just that.

Joe worried about his old friend Henry, living alone out in the desert. He was more worried someone from the new government would find him and try to enlist him in the new country.

Knowing Henry the way he did, Joe could not paint a pretty picture of a confrontation between the old Indian and the new government.

Besides those two, there was no one else from his old life Joe could think about besides Beanie. That last cryptic message from Todd before Joe was knocked into the next year had been the only ray of hope Joe had had in a year.

"She's alive," the message across thousands of miles of Internet had said. It was enough to give Joe a reason to go on living.

As badly as he wanted to find her, he could not rush headlong into something that could end badly for everyone involved. Instead, Joe planned to use the military to help him find his beloved wife.

With all of the technology available to the military and the new government, Joe would surely be able to locate Beanie. The only problem was getting to a position where he could utilize the military's unrestricted use of restricted information.

To do this, Joe would have to build the trust of his superiors. Going to the border detail without a protest was a stepping-stone on the way to his ultimate goal of finding a place in logistics.

Logistics was the brain of the military. Who and when were important, but the most crucial element of all things military was the where. If Joe could get to the information locked inside the military's databases, he could locate everyone involved in his life.

Weighing heavily on him was his own role in the chaos. He had never in his life hid behind the it's-not-my-fault philosophy that many people adopted. He was responsible for everything touching his life, in one form or another. The deaths of loved ones, friends, and strangers were the worst.

The thought that he might be the only person in the world who had the knowledge to make things right was a burden no man should have to bear. In addition to making things right within his own life, he had a heavy obligation to make things right in the world.

He had narrowly escaped his own death so many times he had become immune to the fear of dying. His only save from a total death-wish was the vengeance that still burned within him. His guilt over the world's present condition was secondary.

Once Joe was in logistics, his next step would be overseas deployment. He had already planned to get back to Europe by hook or crook, but it would be much better if he could step on foreign soil legitimately within the protection of the military. Of course, once there he would go AWOL so that he could finally finish his unfinished business.

All great plans are great until they start to unravel. Joe's unraveled as soon as he bumped into an old friend from his not too distant past.

Joe was walking through downtown Dallas with some of the men from his unit. This new military required its recruits to police their designated areas as a form of public awareness that Joe guessed was a way of telling the population the military was the real power in the States.

As they were walking through downtown, Joe saw a familiar face that jolted him from present to past in a millisecond. How Dr. Tanaki ended up hundreds of miles from the town where it had all come apart for Joe was a question foremost on Joe's mind when he crossed the street and grabbed the unsuspecting doctor by the arm.

Dr. Tanaki's eyes widened and he paled briefly before

the blood rushed back into his face. When his arm was taken in a firm grasp from behind, the first thought that crossed Miko's mind was that Vincent had found him again.

When he saw it was another type of ghost from his past, he almost wept in relief. In ways he was a very strong man, but in others he was simply a man whose emotions were never far from the surface.

"Joe!" he exclaimed as he quickly turned and hugged the haggard man before him. "Joe!" he exclaimed again, almost joyfully, as he hugged him again.

The first thought running through Miko's mind was how much he needed to explain to Joe about the night Joe's wife was murdered. He had planned to get to Joe somehow after his arrest and try to tell him he knew that the person Joe had killed had not been Beanie.

Before he had a chance to talk to Joe, Joe had escaped and gone on the run. After a brief manhunt, the entire case was taken over by a department within the government that no one had ever heard of.

Within two days of the murder, the case was wrapped up so tightly under the guise of national security that any mention of Joe or Beanie brought a pair or more of cold-eyed men from this unknown governmental branch. Their questioning and menacing demeanor was so intense that within a week after the murder, no one in the normally laid-back town dared mention Joe or Beanie again.

"Joe, there's so much I need to talk to you about," Miko continued. "I know you didn't kill Beanie. I know it because I know what that thing was you killed. Joe, we have to talk, but not here, not here."

Joe smiled at Miko. He remembered how excited the alcoholic coroner could become when something out the mundane happened. He also remembered the doctor's reaction when he had lifted the dead woman's hair as she lay in the pool of blood on Joe's floor.

It had been like he had seen a rattlesnake about to strike.

Joe remembered Dr. Tanaki scurrying back and almost slipping in the congealing blood on the floor. He remembered Tanaki's ghostly white face and dilated eyes, sure signs of shock.

Joe had tucked all those memories in the extraordinary compartment inside his mind that held everything from his first awareness to the present. His blessing and curse was that horrible or wonderful ability to recall, in minute detail, everything his eyes had ever seen and anything his ears had ever heard.

Joe looked back at his unit waiting across the street. Although none of the men were suspicious – all had run across one person or another they knew from their old lives on their daily street beats – Joe did not want to raise anyone's eyes.

"Quick, what's your number?" Joe asked. Miko told him his number and Joe committed it, of course, to memory. Their encounter on the street was over in less than a minute, but in Joe's state of mind, it had lasted too long.

12.

The focus of the new Untied States of the Americas was securing the nation's power structure within its borders and increasing these same borders by force. Conquering new territory was second for the hungry new government. The United States of the Americas' insatiable appetite would not be satiated until the entire world became part of the nation.

It was not so far off. The Franco-Germanic coalition was in trouble. Larger forces had crossed the Mediterranean from the Saudi coalition in Northern Africa and they had caught the French and Germans by surprise.

A Chinese-Indian army had overrun most of Russia by means of superior weapons and strategies. The only part of Russia that was holding out was the cold northeastern corner of Siberia. The extreme temperatures seemed to be that area's only true defense.

Russia appealed to the States and the States responded out of self-preservation. If China overtook the Siberian corner of Russia, it was only a matter of time before their forces crossed the Bering Strait into the States.

An enormous force, bigger than any that had ever been mobilized in military history, stepped on the frozen tundra of the Russian territory within forty-eight hours of Russia's request for help. Most of the men from the force were selected from harsh, cold areas in the States and the former Canada – these men and women were used to bitter cold.

With better weapons than the alleged superior weaponry of the Chinese, and the ability of the States' forces to adapt quickly to the frigid conditions (most of the soldiers deployed to Siberia were used to zero degrees, anyway), the Chinese were overrun and pushed back to the southern areas of their original nation within a week.

Along the way, the United States of the Americas claimed Russian and northern Chinese territory for its own. Although not part of the continental States, the new territory would be easily controlled by establishing a tremendously large "peace-keeping" force throughout Russia and northern China.

The new States were ruthless. Any who did not conform were exterminated. To justify their actions, the overseas military told the people at home it was for their own protection.

In part, this was true. But, another insidious reason was because men meant less than land, and physical territory was infinitely more important than mere people.

The new States did not waste time on the pleasantries of war, such as negotiations and prisoners. The time for treaties was over for the States; war became war and the main focus was conquest.

Like conquerors of old, each superpower looked only to increase their territory and rule it by coercion or brutality. The States were no different.

When a pocket of resistance continued to be a thorn in its side during the Russian Wars, the States pulled out the heavy guns – the newly developed weapons of last resort, the A-guns.

Scientists and weaponologists in the States had been working twenty-four hours a day once the first superpower battles began. The new gun was actually from an old theory developed by German scientists during World War II.

By harnessing the power of the atom in a miniature, stable nuclear reactor, the developers in the States were able to create the first atom bomb gun. A slight change in the molecular structure made the A-gun's ammunition harmless to the shooter. It also made the nuclear component controllable: one could remotely set the detonation time and the total area to eradicate.

A sonic buffer emanated from the gun, preventing a backlash of nuclear particles. Once the target field was established, the nuclear reactor released its destructive power within a contained area.

The gun was twice the size of an AK-47 and three times its weight, but it was portable and easy to set up. An A-gun could be ready to go within ten minutes. Its portability made the weapon's power of destruction worse than the actual atom bomb.

On the third day of the Russian Wars, a twenty-three square mile stretch inside China's northeastern corner was laid to waste within minutes. Nothing was left alive, neither man, mammal, or plant. The only thing that remained was a pungent three-foot layer of dust covering a once vital and alive area.

The defining feature of the new A-gun was its ability to create a controlled burn. The settings allowed the user to determine how many square inches, feet, or miles to release the atomic energy. Once the burn reached its preset limit, it collapsed in on itself.

A major drawback, however, was the unpredictability of the gun's destructive blowback of radioactive particles in more humid climates. Tests in areas with more moisture revealed that fallout from the nuclear particles rode piggyback on water droplets in the air and could not be contained. The A-gun was more suited and better controlled in dry, cold conditions.

The implications of a destructive force that mimicked something alive were at the same time terrible and exciting.

Three of the A-guns had been released and five others were in development. A special force within the military guarded the plans and designs for the A-guns. Even the scientists and weaponologists never saw the complete plans. Instead, the bits and pieces were put together in stages by different groups.

The States would destroy the plans and all those associated with the A-guns before it would let them fall into the hands of a hostile. Until the last gun was assembled, all workers in the A-gun department were also closely guarded within a special compound. The workers were "special guests" of the military and their enforced stay was a type of incarceration.

Weapons of "Last Resort" were what the A-guns became unofficially known as. Besides obliterating living humans and mammals, they also destroyed land and made it unfit for human habitation for decades.

Land, land, land. That's what it always boiled down to. Living beings, intelligent beings, were always expendable. In the past, the States had kept a low profile on its unfeeling grab for land, regardless of the consequences.

In the time of the chaos, the States only cared about the appearance of strength. To foreign nations outside of the States' coalition, acquisition by force by the United States of the Americas simply reaffirmed what had been thought for decades: America was only waiting for the right moment to achieve world domination.

Now, all the big dogs were on the loose and fighting for the right to be emperor of it all. Masks of diplomacy and cooperation between nations had been stripped away and the only thing left was the ugly face of power.

Controlling newly acquired territories proved easier for the States than had been thought. Most of the conquered and oppressed people welcomed a change in leadership, hoping for changes in their own lives. Often, the leadership change was never a good thing for the population. With the new States, however, it was.

Suddenly, people in poverty had help and food and medical care. Political prisoners were quickly released and, by appealing to their ideological psyche of fighting for the rights of the indigent, convinced to join the new military. People living in conditions not fit for even the worst human being were given better quarters – usually those confiscated by US forces during rebellions at the start of the chaos.

All in all, the lives of millions improved after the United States of the Americas took over their homelands.

The Russians were too ill equipped and too tired from too many wars prior to the chaos. Their alliance with the nation that was once their sworn enemy was nothing short of an anomaly.

They, and other countries like them, benefited from a union with the powerful entity the United States of the Americas was evolving into. An abundance of food, no energy shortages, health care for the masses, better standards of living – it was a very attractive pipe dream to the war-weary people of oppressed foreign countries.

And if their leaders disagreed with the people? The people simply eliminated them and, with welcoming arms, opened their countries up to the States.

At the rate the States were going, they would control the world within short order.

But, the best plans are often fraught with setbacks. The shit hit the fan shortly after the Russian Wars.

While the States had been busy with their conquest of Eastern Europe, the South Afrikaners had been steadily gaining momentum and territory. Wresting the western and central parts of Africa from the Saudis, the South Afrikaners took that victory and branched across the South Atlantic Ocean into Argentina.

When the States' new allies in Russia joined the Afrikaners in their quest for territory, the fluidity of shifting alliances caught the United States of the Americas off-guard. It really pissed the States' government off that a nation they had just bailed out had turned on them within a matter of days.

Not only that, but the Russians had developed their own rudimentary portable nuclear weapon. Though not as compact, safe, or powerful as the States' A-gun, it packed enough of a punch to make it a serious contender.

Meanwhile, the upper United States of the Americas started mobilizing and deploying troops to Brazil, in addition to strengthening coastlines and borders. All military personnel were on high alert and CEUs across the country were indoctrinated into a type of homeland army.

Joe's unit was one of the first sent to the Brazilian border. Because of his prior military training and experience, Joe was promoted and put in charge of an elite guerilla unit. This newly formed group was given the dangerous assignment of reconnaissance behind enemy lines.

Déjà vu. Joe felt like he had stepped back a decade to his mercenary days. The humid climate, the hiding and waiting, the blitz attacks. In and out, just like the old days.

His unit was equally qualified to follow his lead into jungle warfare. Abraham, or Abba for short, had been a logistics operator for an illegal import/export company. He redeemed himself, and shortened his prison sentence, when he volunteered for duty in the first Brazilian Wars. His special ability to accurately measure distances to within a few inches and volume within ounces – all without special equipment – made him a valuable asset to Joe's group.

Other members of the Congo Force unit were equally skilled: Jackson was an expert navigator who used the stars as his primary guide and held a master's degree in astronomy. Heff, a former bookkeeper for a Fortune 500 Company, held the coordinates of every member of the unit in his mind. Rock, a champion video game player, was a precision attack specialist. Rounding out the group was Elk, a hulking giant of a man, who was an expert at long-range targeting and close combat pummeling.

Joe's head was still reeling from this sudden change in his life. Only a few days before, he had been walking the streets of Dallas with another military unit. Life for Joe was mimicking his military days where situations changed from day to day, and, sometimes, from minute to minute.

Now, he was in command of a unit charged with targeting an enemy that had not been an enemy a week ago. The dizzying changes in alliances was enough to make anyone's head spin, but, like most things in life, people got used to whatever the people in charge told them to.

As Joe was crouching in position in a wet forest in Argentina, he thought about Dr. Tanaki. Seeing the doctor on the streets of Dallas just a few days before had reminded Joe of his old life before it had collapsed.

It was curious that the doctor was in Dallas. From what he remembered of the man, he preferred his privacy and calm, predictable life with patients who did not talk back, as he had often told anyone who would listen, to the hectic pace of a big city and a practice with patients who were physically alive.

Joe had tried to call the doctor before he left, but had

only gotten his answering machine. Part of him regretted that he had not had a chance to talk to Dr. Tanaki before he left, but, the other part was relieved, because seeing the doctor brought memories of the terrible time in Joe's past life to the surface.

Not that Joe ever forgot killing the woman who was pretending to be his wife, but he had a place he kept those memories in his mind, behind a door he kept closed. When anything triggered them, his sadness at his lost life threatened to overwhelm him.

The heat and humidity of the jungle was invading every inch of Joe's fatigues and every crack and crevice of his skin. The sweat dripping from his hair had soaked through the absorbent wrap he had tied around his forehead.

As he silently griped about the conditions, he heard a rustling from the brush twenty feet away. Slowly turning and leveling his gun, Joe released the safety with a flick of his thumb and took aim at the spot.

A wild baby boar poked its head out from underneath a bush and quickly scooted across the overgrown path Joe was crouched next to. As Joe relaxed, he almost missed the man following the boar.

In fatigues similar to Joe's, the man could have passed for a fellow soldier. What gave him away, and what Joe immediately noticed, was the insignia on his uniform was not in English.

Drawing his weapon, the foreign soldier did not have time to raise it more than two inches before Joe shot him point-blank in the chest. Jumping up with combat knife in hand, Joe quickly covered the soldier's mouth with one hand and slit his throat with the other. His dying gurgle tickled the palm of Joe's hand.

Joe quietly killed, but it was already too late. Even though his gun had a silencer, the small sound from the recoil had given his position away. The unit's position had been extremely compromised.

Pulling back while motioning for the others in Congo Force to do the same, Joe had no time to assess the enemy's location or strength. He only knew that the bullets flying around them would eventually find their mark if the unit did not haul ass out of there.

Crouching low and running hard, Joe heard a sharp grunt and then a curse. Whipping his head around, he saw Elk crouched on one knee, holding his side as blood seeped between his fingers.

Reversing direction, Joe ran back toward Elk. Grabbing his arm, Joe struggled to help the three-hundred and fifty pound Goliath back up on his feet. As the pair ran, Joe's chest was heaving with the effort to support Elk and to keep up with the unit.

As Congo Force covered more distance between themselves and the enemy, the sound of shots faded away. Somehow, they had lost their enemies in the brush. Joe was not getting his hopes up, though. If they stopped, it would only be a matter of time before the enemy found them.

When the unit broke through the heavy brush, Joe could just make out the sound of a helicopter coming in from the east. He knew the noise would draw soldiers from the other side. Hugging the edge of the small clearing, the unit watched for enemies as their transport touched down.

"Oh, shit," Joe said as he saw who the pilot was.

Of all the ghosts from his past, he never thought he would run into "Loco" Matisse. Loco had been the helicopter pilot during Joe's mercenary days and he hadn't come by that nickname for nothing.

As a daredevil god trapped in the body of a mere mortal, Loco had constantly defied the bond and bounds of what it was to be human. He had once taken a helicopter into a tailspin on purpose to prove that only idiots could not break out of the spiraling death.

One time, he had flown only a few feet off the ground for miles without hitting anything and another time, he had swerved in and out of the busy streets of Oklahoma City, barely missing mailboxes, telephone wires, and traffic.

There was nothing he would not do on a dare or for money. Joe wondered what the hell Loco was doing in the military and why he had not been psyched out from the start.

"Slap my monkey," Loco said. "If it isn't Beanpole Joe!"

Laughing, Loco climbed down from the pilot's chair and gave Joe a bear hug. Joe quickly hugged him back, and said, "We gotta get out of here, now."

"Dude, I'm on it," Loco said as he hopped back in the pilot's chair, powered up, and launched straight up from the grass dirt pad.

13.

People from Joe's past were coming out of the woodwork. Some were coming out from under rocks.

If anyone had asked, Joe would have told them that Loco Matisse had to be dead because no one could have escaped near-death as many times as Loco. From his escapades with helicopters to his ability to pick women with big, mean husbands or boyfriends, it was amazing Loco was still walking the earth.

After they had landed at base camp inside the safe zone of Sao Borja, Brazil, Joe made his way to the front of the helicopter.

"Man, what are you doing here?" Loco asked as he checked his gauges. "The last I saw of you was after we got back to camp from that Mosquito Alley fubar. I figured you must be dead or something."

"I've been busy," Joe answered.

"Me, too, man. I was busy serving time after I accidentally hit a cop's car."

Joe gave Loco a puzzled look and said, "I used to be a cop. Unless you were drunk or high, you wouldn't normally go to jail just for an accident with a police car."

"Yeah, I know," Loco said with a grin. "I accidentally hit him with my bird and knocked his top-lights off. They took one look at my bad-ass record and threw me in with the common riff-raff."

"Loco, I don't know what to say," Joe laughed. "Except, they must have seen something good in you to let you out and in a bird again."

"Yeah, they saw how crazy I am and thought I'd be safer away from them and out in this jungle hell." Loco paused to grab his logbook as he headed out the helicopter. "Come on, let's go get a drink and talk about the bad old times."

"I'll meet you later, man," Joe said as he and Abba helped Elk off the helicopter. Elk's weight seemed to have tripled during the flight to base.

"You gotta lose some weight, man, if you plan on getting shot a lot," Abba said. "You're too fat for me to be lugging your lazy ass around."

Elk grinned, then groaned. As Joe and Abba struggled under his mass, the other members of Congo Force tried to help, but Joe waved them off. He did not want to lose any more than two men if Elk was to go down.

After Joe and Abba settled Elk into the infirmary, they each went their separate ways. Joe was not sure how much trouble he would eventually get into if he had that first drink with Loco, but curiosity got the better of him as he headed out toward the camp's makeshift bar.

It was hot and humid in the tented building. The lukewarm beer knocked the dust and grime out of Joe's throat. After the second one, he began to relax.

Listening to Loco, Joe realized his crazy friend did not know anymore about their old mercenary group than he did. Apparently, when the group disbanded, Loco returned to his old stomping ground, Los Angeles, and starting getting into trouble after trouble.

What did make Joe's ears perk up was when Loco starting talking about the trouble in Europe. A lot of what he was saying did not make sense, which he expected since it was Loco talking. But, a little bit of what Loco said eerily matched what Joe already knew to be true.

"Yeah, they said that the Chaos started in Austria and Switzerland," Loco started. "Something about some guy was supposed to be keeping everybody in line, but he bit the big one. Or maybe it was some queen bee. I don't rightly remember."

Loco took a huge gulp of his beer and wiped his mouth on the back of his hand. "All I know is that everything went to shit real quick and beer don't taste the same anymore."

Joe sat and listened to Loco talk about how things had really changed – or, at least, how they had changed from Loco's point of view. According to Loco, there was a vast conspiracy and only a few were in control. The Chinese had spiked all the water in the world with PCP. There had only been one president, ever, and he was reincarnated every four years at election time.

Loco's ramblings sounded just like Loco, Joe thought as he grinned into his beer. Some things never changed.

"What I don't get is why we can't get good German beer. I don't care what war we're in, it's a damned crime that I can't get my favorite beer unless I join the German army."

Joe listened a little while longer and eased his way out of the make-shift bar when Loco's ramblings became more delusional as his beer intake increased. It felt just like old times.

The days that followed Congo Force's botched surveillance attempt were a little more productive. Joe and his men were able to get fixed location sites on three enemy sites. With the sites targeted, Congo Force stealthily seeded the enemy's camp.

Detonating the explosives set at the first camp from a distance, Congo's elite shootists were able to pick off any enemy soldiers who had escaped the deadly force of the bombs. They did not stand a chance.

The second camp was more of the same. The explosive charges did their work and whatever was left after the deadly blasts, Joe's crew took care of. The foreign soldiers lay dead or dying in humid fields far from their homelands.

Climbing onto a ridge overlooking the third camp, Joe and his unit were already thinking of the beer they were ready to have as soon as they got back to base camp. Nothing was any different about this last camp, but as they were setting off the explosives, all hell broke loose behind them.

Out of the dank, dense forest, a force of thousands erupted. Joe watched in disbelief as the large force of enemy soldiers hunkered down behind trees and brush in preparation for battle.

Even before Joe yelled for Heff to find out what the hell was going on, Heff was on the radio to base. No one responded.

"Wanker bella two, this is CF one, come in," Heff

repeated over and over again, for at least a dozen times as he and the others in Congo Force swiftly retreated.

There was still no response and that could only mean one of two things: base had retreated ahead of the massive enemy force and sacrificed Joe's unit hoping to slow the enemy down long enough for the bulk of the base to escape or the base had been destroyed.

Although it did not seem possible that such a force could have landed undetected, Joe was not above believing anything could happen. In the case of the States' New Military, their arrogant superiority complex felt that nothing would escape their notice, but all it would take would be one soldier asleep at the wheel for the entire house of cards to fall down.

Slipping into an area under the radar was another possibility and Joe had had extensive experience doing just that. It was amazingly easy to find and exploit the weak points in a country's defenses.

Regardless, these thoughts were fleeting in Joe's mind as he and his unit fled their position ahead of the enemy. His only concern, now, was how the dick were they going to get out without air support?

Their initial drop had been on a high ridge two miles from the first target point. With no one answering Heff's increasingly frantic calls, it was starting to seem that a helicopter lift was out of the question.

Instead, it looked like they were in for some fast, hard, and heavy marching through unfamiliar territory as Joe steered everyone toward the northeastern border. If nothing else, they had to determine what might have happened to base camp and then they could reassess their situation.

Ahead, Abba stopped suddenly and held up his hand. As he slipped into the brush alongside the trail, the others in Congo Force did the same.

Three minutes later, a troop of over one-hundred men, black and white, marched along the same trail Joe and his fellow soldiers had just been on. Eerily silent, the foreign soldiers were on high alert as they marched. The only sound

Joe heard was the commanding officer as he quietly talked on his radio.

Was it a lucky coincidence that Joe's unit almost ran into a very organized and very large group of South Afrikaners? Joe did not think so. Not with the way the soldiers were scanning the area, as if they were looking for something. Or someone, like an elite American targeting team.

After the last soldier passed, Joe's unit waited. As jungle mosquitoes the size of hummingbirds buzzed his face, Joe could think of a hundred other places he would rather be.

Fifteen minutes after the last soldier passed, a smaller unit marched by. These soldiers were the trail-backs, and they were the most dangerous. Trail-backs came after the major section of a military unit passed to see if any stray enemies felt safe enough to come out of hiding. Joe's gut had told him to stay put. Good thing he listened instead of passing that funny feeling off as gas.

Eight minutes after the trail-backs passed by, the unit heard the whomp-whomp sound of a helicopter coming out of the north. Waving Abba down as he was standing up to signal the low-flying helicopter, Joe pointed to his eyes and then to the sky. Wait and watch.

It was not a friendly. The distinctive insignia on the side of the transport helicopter was foreign. As the helicopter passed over Congo Force's hiding place, everyone felt exposed. Although they were well-hidden on the ground with the dense brush surrounding them, from the air they were sitting ducks.

After the helicopter passed, Joe and his crew took to a back trail along the creek to the east. As Jackson looked at the sky and then the map in his hand, he motioned for the unit to head across the creek when they were about four miles into their hike.

Coming upon another trail, Congo Force redoubled their efforts to quickly get to base camp and try to sort through everything. All Joe knew for sure was that intelligence and strategic reports they should have received about enemy locations had not been there for them. Logistics had failed miserably.

Throughout the night, Congo Force walked, ran, and crawled their way through the humid overgrown land toward their base. All the men were thinking the same thing, but none wanted to bring it up: base had not responded to any of their communications on every frequency on their radio.

That could only mean one of three things: the camp was under total radio silence, the camp had been destroyed, or the entire camp had retreated. The latter two were ominous.

A hazy dawn broke through the trees. The filtered light made the forest look gloomy and depressing, and did nothing to lift anyone's spirits. Rock in particular was dragging his feet behind the rest of the guys and Joe had to turn back a few times to hurry him up.

Coming in from the west, Congo Force came upon the first enemy outpost within a half mile from base camp. The unfortunate lookout faced south toward the bulk of the States' military action. Rock climbed stealthily through the brush and garroted the lone guard, who obliged Rock by quickly and quietly dying.

The second lookout was only a hundred yards from the destroyed camp. As Joe looked around with heat sensitive binoculars, he spotted four additional outposts. Other than that, the destroyed camp was deserted.

Leaving lookouts around an annihilated stronghold was an age-old tactical war maneuver. Any straggling soldiers would always try to get back to the original launch pad of an operation. The enemy would be able to pick them off, one by one.

Joe handed the binoculars to Abba, who, after seeing the lookouts for himself, handed them to Heff. Instantly plotting the distance to each outpost, Heff turned to Rock, quietly gave him the logistics for the attack, and the tactical assault specialist scribbled the numbers in the notebook he had been using to keep track of wins and losses from the unit's nightly Texas Holdem

Setting up his Predator II SRAW, Rock knew he would only have seconds between his attacks. The good thing about the second version of the short-range assault weapon was its ability to set multiple target coordinates. The weapon's range could be flipped as the next missile was being loaded.

The rest of the crew spread out to make themselves less of a target should any of the enemy survive and try to return fire. Separated by thirty yards, each member trained their guns on one or the other of the enemy outposts.

As Joe crouched on one knee and trained his gun on one of the outposts at the northern edge of the camp, he felt the pit of his stomach flipping as it sank home that they were on their own. The New Military had deserted them without so much as a warning.

Rock started the barrage of death. Quickly reloading, he kept his eyes on the assault weapon's coordinates and adjusted them rapidly in between targets. Within thirty seconds, all of the outposts had been destroyed.

Joe and his men waited in their hiding places for any survivors. With the power behind Rock's Predator, Joe doubted any could have lived through the assault missiles.

Congo Force held its position for an hour. Joe and Abba checked the camp every five minutes, but nothing moved. The burning outposts continued to burn and Joe could see the scorched, dismembered bodies of some of the foreign soldiers within the perimeters of their former posts.

Cautiously, Joe and Abba approached their former base camp. As they looked around, they found the bullet-ridden bodies of some of their former comrades. Inside the communications hut, all the equipment had been destroyed.

Their fellow soldiers inside the infirmary had not had a chance to fight back. All were dead, shot in the beds where they had been recuperating.

Joe had stepped into the infirmary fully expecting to find Elk's body. When Joe and his crew had left Elk two days before, the big man was still trying to get back on his feet after having surgery to remove the bullets in his chest.

Elk was not among the dead. Joe had no explanation other than he had escaped either with the bulk of the soldiers stationed at base camp or had left on his own. It looked like the dead men in the infirmary had not been given a thought when the entire camp retreated.

Given Elk's injuries, Joe seriously doubted he would have been able to keep up with the others. On second thought, Elk may not have been able to strike out on his own with the injuries he was recovering from.

The third option? Elk had hunkered down somewhere close, probably in a makeshift cave, licking his wounds like an animal. Although he had never said, Joe had the feeling that Elk may have been a mercenary, too. It takes one to know one.

After Abba and Joe scouted the camp, Joe signaled the others. The unit walked the camp and salvaged what little they could. Joe was looking through some maps that had survived when his telecom unit beeped.

"Forty-two, alpha george. Congo teams, come in," a voice called through the static.

"Switch," Joe replied quietly into the mouthpiece.

Joe knew the security frequency that was being used the day he and his unit had marched into the jungle, but if the channel had changed during the past two days, he was sunk.

Switching to the last coded frequency he knew, Joe was relieved to hear forty-two, alpha george counting down until he jumped off the assigned channel.

"Congo Force twenty. Come in, alpha george," Joe spoke.

"That you, Beanpole Joe?"

Joe laughed sharply when he heard Loco's voice. My life is full of mystery and irony, Joe thought for the hundredth time.

"Get to coordinates 32.5 and 55.3. I'll be waiting for you, but if you don't see me it means the boogie men ate me."

Joe did not understand the last part of what Loco said, but he did not really care. The thought of rescue was a relief and gave Joe just a glimmer of hope that he and the others would get out of this alive.

He needed to get out. He had been trapped in the

military only as a means of gaining entry into their database. Being shipped to South America had been an unwelcome side trip, but one that he could not get out of without repercussions.

There was nothing more important than finding his wife and holding accountable, with extreme vengeance, the men in charge of fucking up his and Beanie's lives. Since he had received Todd's message that she was still alive, it had eaten at him that he had been hindered by so many things and stopped at so many turns in his quest to find Beanie.

Thoughts of getting back to the States had never been far from his mind, but he never imagined it would be like this. To be on the run and dependent on a somewhat crazy helicopter pilot for rescue was one ball that had been hit out of the park.

14.

Before Congo Force left the deserted base camp, Elk emerged from hiding. The big man shuffled slowly toward the crew and Joe could tell that he was hurting.

Abba was the first to reach him and helped him sit down on the ground. Heff went back to the infirmary to see if he could find any more medications that might have been overlooked.

"It's good to see you, Elk," Joe told the weary man. "How bad?"

"I can make it," Elk grimaced. "Bullet's out, but it's infected."

"Don't worry, man," Joe reassured him. "We're getting out of here and we'll get you to a hospital stateside."

"It came out of nowhere," Elk began without any prompting from Joe. "Short range bogeys and air dumps. Then, those bitches started crawling out of the forest."

Elk paused to take a sip of water from the canteen Abba offered him. "No warning, man. When the first dump hit, it took half the camp out. I crawled under the medi-tent and trenched down outside the perimeter. I could see everything going on and they wasn't taking no prisoners, man. If it moved, they shot it."

"What happened to communications?" Heff asked as he joined the group.

"They knocked that out with that first dump," Elk replied. "After they exterminated the camp, they set up those outposts." Elk grinned slightly at Rock. "That was some fine shooting, Tex."

"Can you walk? We've got about five klicks to go to get to a helicopter pickup," Joe told Elk.

"I'll make it," Elk said as he slowly got to his feet.

"Take these," Heff told Elk as he took some tablets out of his front pocket. "One's for the rot and the others are white rabbits."

Joe looked at Heff and Heff shrugged. "Hey,

somebody's gonna make off with them, so why not us?"

"Point," Joe answered.

Elk chewed the tablets and washed them down with more water. Groaning, he pushed himself to his feet and joined the others.

The five klicks to the helicopter rendezvous felt more like twenty, especially to Elk. The dense undergrowth impeded their trek and the loose dirt and rock of the trail slowed them down as their feet fought for traction.

Quietness prevailed, however. The men moved silently through the forest and, at one point, moved off the overgrown trail when they heard voices. They watched as locals walked to the south, their arms loaded with looted goods from a New Military supply truck.

Finally, Congo Force arrived at the helicopter's landing point. Crouching on the outside perimeter, Joe quietly told his men to be ready to run as soon as the helicopter touched down.

Twenty minutes passed the agreed upon time that Loco had given him. Joe did not have a Plan B – if Loco did not show up, Joe had no way to get back to friendly territory, especially with a wounded Elk.

Of course, the uppers Elk had taken were helping him considerably. He was feeling no pain and had had more strength and stamina than some of the rest of his fellow grunts. He was in for a big crash, though, and Joe needed to be on friendly ground when that happened.

The thought of trying to carry Elk made him shudder.

Rock was the first to hear the helicopter in the distance. As it got closer and closer, the men were on higher alert. If the enemy was in the vicinity, there would be a serious fight.

Loco touched down. With Elk leading the way, Congo Force ran toward the helicopter. Before the last man was fully in, Loco was taking off. If Jackson had not grabbed Abba's hand, he would have fallen back to the ground.

Joe went to the front and sat beside Loco in the empty co-pilot's seat.

"Where's your partner?" he asked.

"Man, he bailed out when that shit started. He's probably dead on the ground somewhere."

"How far can we get," Joe asked.

Loco looked as his gauges. "At least to the old Mexican border, but don't worry. There's a way station there and another one close by where I can refuel.

"How far are you wanting to go, anyway?"

Joe was not ready to tell Loco what he had been tossing over and over in his mind.

Most importantly, Joe needed to find Beanie. Secondly, Joe needed to try to find Henry and Todd. After that, he was going to Europe to the place where it had all started.

"We need to get to a station with a database," Joe answered instead.

A few hours later, Loco touched down at a deserted Columbian base outside of Pereira. Refueling quickly, they were back in the air within twenty minutes.

Loco headed west toward the coast once they crossed the border into Mexico. He explained to Joe that it looked like, from the little he could tell, that whatever huge force had invaded had landed on the eastern coast.

"Where is everyone?" Joe wondered out loud as they passed over another deserted United States base.

"They just scattered when the shit started flying," Loco answered. "No nothing from higher up; it was every man for himself."

Loco laughed ironically. "Look at how the great American military just fell apart. Everybody cut and ran when the shit hit. This damn military ain't like what we had, Joe. It's full of sissy boys and accountants."

"Hey, I heard that, asshole," Rock called from the back. "At least I can count how many beers I've had, unlike you, you moron."

"Oh, shit," Joe heard Loco say under his breath. Just as they passed over the American base near Caborca, Loco suddenly turned back south. Joe looked the north where Loco pointed and saw the faintest glint in the sky.

"Flyers coming in, heading due south, and there," Loco

said as he pointed to the west. "Don't want to wait around to see if they're ours or theirs. I'm flying low, but they still might spot me."

Forever. That was the first thought that crossed Joe's mind. It was going to take forever to get back to the States.

Joe did not have forever. He had been going nonstop for over a year and his mind and body were wearing out. Even with brief respites, Joe was exhausted, mentally and physically.

He had looked at his reflection in the mirror of the makeshift bathroom in base camp four days before. He had really looked, not just glanced at himself like he normally did. He had stopped looking a long time before because the sight of his dead eyes unnerved him.

This time, he had stared. There were deep wrinkles that hadn't been there before and grey strands were swiftly overtaking his coal-black hair. His face was gaunt and tense, and lines that hadn't been there before were becoming more prominent with each passing day.

He had aged dramatically in a very short time. His body had telltale painful signs. His jaw ached, despite the fact that it had not really been broken. His feet still hurt from running over broken ground during his escape from Normal. If he had to list every ache and pain, well, he could write a book.

Something besides the way he felt made him feel his time was short. He could not put his finger on it, but he felt that everything was coming to a head.

Snapping out of his reverie, Joe asked Loco to repeat himself.

"I said, we're gonna have to set down for a bit 'til those flyers go by."

Loco pointed to his left. "I don't want to keep heading the same direction they're going. Just gonna have to lay low for a bit. Don't wanna get boxed in."

The hours on the ground passed slowly. Everyone stayed on alert, watching the area around the helicopter. Since evening was fast approaching, the unit hunkered down for the night with two men taking guard duty on a rotating three-hour basis.

At first light, Congo Force loaded up and prepared to cross the border into the States. Maintaining an open radio frequency, Heff continued to broadcast their call sign, but there was no response.

It seemed the New Military had left the building.

Without military discipline, the task of guarding the country may have fallen into the hands of citizens with guns. If that was the case, then citizens would have absolute life and death power.

Not that it was such a bad thing; government had ruled lives for far too long and it was time for the common man to stand up for himself. But, as history told over and over again, in situations where governments fall, dictators and despots usually step in to fill the void of leadership.

Joe thought about these things as they crossed the Mexican border into the homeland. Along the way, they had not seen any active military units. The only thing they had seen were the destroyed remnants of deserted bases.

"I'm open frequency, but, nothing, man, nothing," Rock told Joe. "I'm talking to dead air."

Joe nodded. He did not need to say out loud what they were all thinking: with no radio contact in over twenty-four hours, the outlook was ominous. As quickly as the new United States of the Americas had overtaken other countries, their own country itself may have been conquered.

It was a chilling thought.

An hour over the border, Loco touched down at Kirtland Air Force Base near the White Sand Missile Range outside of Alamogordo, New Mexico. Refueling in the eerily silent base, the crew stayed on high alert for anyone who might stop them. As far as they were concerned, anyone with a gun, military, civilian, or anything in between, was a potential enemy.

Earlier, Joe had told Loco about Red Dusk, an Army shadow base thirty miles south of Farmington. Heading northwest after refueling and leaving the ghost base, they touched down just one hour northwest of Kirtland.

Red Dusk was not on any map. Like hundreds of smaller bases throughout the States, Red Dusk operated off the grid. A shadow base, like Red Dusk, was characterized by tighter security, higher fences, and elite soldiers charged with full-response defense.

Regular grunts in the military knew nothing about shadow bases. For the most part, these hidden-in-broad-daylight camps were stand-alones with all of the equipment and technology needed to function on their own.

Occasionally, a shadow base was exposed. When that happened, it was fronted as a supply and maintenance base for a larger base nearby. Although rare, these blown covers did not slow the shadow soldiers down – they simply established a new base in another area.

Only about twenty percent of enlisted and commissioned soldiers knew what the shadows really were. Even most higher ranking officers knew nothing about these bases – the secrets remained with the hardcore, true military men.

Sarge had known. One of the things Joe and Liz had discussed during the three weeks they were at the survivalists' camp was the existence of the bases. Sarge had trusted his daughter with the a map of the locations of the secret installations that he knew of. Unfortunately, it had been in her "sanctuary" house during the Muveed attack.

Liz remembered some of them and pinpointed them on a map for Joe. That was all it took – Joe did not have to look at the map again. Like everything he had ever seen, the map imprinted itself on his mind.

As he gave Loco the coordinates to the shadow camp near the northern New Mexico border, he wondered what they would find. The best would be if other soldiers were there – friendlies, of course. The worst? That would be if it was already in the hands of the enemy and Congo Force was captured or killed.

Along the way, Loco and Joe spotted a rag-tag group of armed people. If renegade soldiers and citizens with guns were what they were going to be up against, Joe thought, then it would be prudent to steer as far away from the unpredictable militia as possible.

"Evasive, now, Loco," he told the pilot.

The crowd on the ground continued to watch the helicopter. Loco swung to the east to throw them off their trail. There was no telling what conditions might be waiting at the shadow camp, but they did not need to add to it by having unpredictable gunslingers following them.

Many of the shadow bases were undetectable from the air. The buildings were not underground; rather, the building itself became part of the landscape. In northern New Mexico, Joe had to keep a sharp eye out to spot scraggly brush and desert dirt that hid the base from view.

The map Liz had given Joe also had coordinates. When Loco was landing at the longitude and latitude Joe had given him, he had seen nothing from the air. Once on the ground, there was still nothing to be seen unless one knew what to look for.

The camouflage was amazing. From above, it simply looked like hilly desert terrain with patchwork scrub brush. On the ground, the smokescreen was the same with one minor difference: there was a small keypad in a recessed area in an anomaly on the side of the rocky hill.

A generic code was locked into all of the systems' keypads. The latitude, longitude, and state code were all it took to get into the base. Joe did not know what to expect to happen once he keyed in the code. As he punched the numbers into the keypad, he had a fleeting moment of fear that the area might be booby-trapped.

Nothing happened. Joe looked at Heff who was standing beside him and shrugged. Everyone except Elk (who was still doped up) jumped when, a minute after Joe had keyed the code, a loud squeal sounded from the inside.

A small portion of the rocky hill clicked and a cleverly hidden and well concealed door opened an inch. With his AK drawn, Joe stepped forward and opened it wider.

No one rushed them and no bullets were flying around them. They would have to check out the rest of the base carefully, all the while looking for anyone who might have stayed behind to guard it.

As they walked in, the quiet was eerie. Walking through a short tunnel, they suddenly emerged into a typical military base, albeit on a much smaller scale. Since most of the shadow bases now ran on seventy percent solar power, it was no surprise that the lights were blazing in every building that they could see from where they were standing.

The entire base was underground, so the only thing missing was the sun. But, not for long, as Joe looked up to where Jackson was pointing. He could see the infrastructure of a sliding dome, which meant that the base was equipped to handle air transport.

Once they opened the dome, Loco could set his Black Hawk down inside the base. After that, Joe could get down to the business of finding his wife.

15.

In a town not too far from the shadow camp south of Farmington, New Mexico, a man was desperately trying to figure out a way to get out from under the hands of a gang of armed and confused expatriates.

Confused was an understatement. The group was a mixed bag of teachers, bank tellers, fast food workers, cashiers, daycare workers, managers, and other assorted citizens with guns.

It did not matter that Todd was not a true hostage; under the loose code of the group, any member was free to leave at any time for any reason. The rule was supposed to guarantee no repercussions against a citizen who no longer wished to be part of the gang.

However, no one had been inclined to test the rule until the day Todd knew he had to leave. His role within the group was to monitor the military's One-Sega computer tracking module, which marked the official and unofficial locations of all military troops.

Similar to the tracking program he had designed for the government many years before, the One-Sega keep real-time records of deployment positions in addition to keyword flags.

The keyword flags were much more important to Todd than the locations. If anyone entered certain words (which the user could specify), then a satellite would accurately pinpoint their location. So far, he had saved the renegade group four times from capture by their own self-defined enemies.

Being the computer whiz that he was, Todd had manipulated the program to monitor not only their own government and military, but any computer connected to the Internet within the continental United States. Although Todd had firewalled and used proxy servers, every time he logged on, there was a twenty percent chance his own location could be exposed by a programmer who might be almost as smart as Todd himself was.

Yesterday, a pair of special keywords he had programmed the first time he used the One-Sega system had triggered an alert. These keywords had been tied to his old life and the friend he had tried to help before he was busted for hacking into the State of Nebraska's Treasury Department.

Todd's time in the county lockup had been mercifully short, in part, due to the chaos erupting all over the world. The military had recruited him to jack their systems and to hack into other countries' servers and high-level programs.

When it all fell apart within the past week, Todd had cut and run. Along the way, he joined a group of gun-toting misfits who were happy to have a computer expert keeping them one step ahead of the people they paranoidly thought were out to get them.

The alert repeated three more times before the user logged off, but Todd was able to pinpoint an exact location. There was only one person in the entire world who would have used these particular keywords. There was only one person who would have been searching for Abigail Daniels.

Todd did not believe in coincidence. He liked to think he was logic first and logic only, but the odds of his old friend Joe being located a mere twenty miles away made Todd's logic meter grind to a halt. If he had believed in mystical connections, this would certainly have been one.

He was determined to get away and find Joe. Todd could not fight the overwhelming feeling that his destiny (there he went again, believing something other than cold facts) was tied to the man wrongly accused of killing his own wife.

But, trying to convince the rag tags that he needed to be somewhere else besides with them was a problem. The only thing left for him to do was to use his ace in the hole, and he was reluctant play that card.

The only way to get away from the gang would be to send them away from him. During down time, he had been building a small program that mimicked the One-Sega, but with a very tiny difference – the locations pinpointed were munitions dumps, the pot of gold for the renegades.

He had not given them these locations, because, frankly, these people he had aligned himself with scared the shit out of him. All the time waving their guns, they were sometimes more of a danger to themselves than to the enemy. More than half of the group had not picked up a gun before the initialization of the See-You enforcement units springing up all across the country.

The day after he found Joe, he told the group where they could find stockpiled weapons. He lied and told the leaders that he was working on a better munitions locating program and needed to finish it with the computer system on which he had started. None of the group had Todd's expertise in computer technology, so it was easy to snowball them.

Two of the group volunteered to stay behind and act as guards for Todd. However, he waved them off with the excuse that they were needed to carry the treasure of guns that was sure to be at the depository.

As soon as they left, Todd was on the Internet, frantically trying to reach Joe. An hour passed, then two. He was antsy as he waited – his renegade group would be coming back within four hours and they would be mad as hell that the place they had sent them was not a gun depository, but a girdle and brassiere warehouse.

Beep. Todd jumped when the computer signaled a response to his hack. He had programmed it to alert him when the person looking for Beanie logged on.

Todd asked the other user a question – who's cantaloupes were bigger, Dougal's Supermarket or Harrison's One-Stop? The user on the other end answered: Trina's at Dougal's. Only someone from Todd's former town would have known the inside joke about which cashier had the bigger boobs and which supermarket she worked at.

Quid pro quo. The user on the other end asked Todd where Mack had put his knife? Mack had been a fellow computer geek and video game guru. Todd typed: through his PS2. Todd was there the night Mack lost his number one standing in the game he ruled and then, lost his mind. Mack plunged an eight inch hunting knife through his gaming system, giving himself a moderate shock that knocked him out long enough for Todd to call the police.

The next message Todd received were the coordinates of a pick-up zone. With all he had been through in the recent past, Todd's nerves were on not just on edge, they had tumbled down the mountain. In the back of his mind, he worried he was being set up and it was not really Joe he had been talking to, but a faceless enemy. The same faceless enemy that had attacked Joe.

Shaking himself, Todd realized he had been with loonies and conspiracy theorists a little too long. He gathered his things and sat down one last time at the computer.

Todd downloaded the tricked-out One-Sega program he had been working on into his portable flash drive. Next, he downloaded the most vicious computer virus he knew. He did not want any of those crazy gun-slinging, sons-of-bitches he had been hanging with to have access to anything more dangerous than themselves.

Then, he took all of the weapons they had left and dumped them in the septic tank behind the building. If they ever found him, the gang would shoot him on sight just for that.

He had twenty minutes to get to the rendezvous point. After walking for fifteen, Todd starting wondering if what he was doing was such a good idea, however, the live-by-the-gun, die-by-the-gun creed of the nuts he just left was not one he shared.

He was hot and sweaty, and he did not see anyone for miles. The dried scrub was not high enough to hide a child, much less a man. The craggy hills were bare of any grass or trees. For miles, there was emptiness. By now, he should have seen someone, but, turning completely around, he saw nothing.

Todd stopped and checked his bearings. He was in the area where Joe was supposed to meet him. Looking around again, he did not see anything or anyone.

Fifteen minutes passed. Todd was starting to feel like he

had been set up when, from behind, a hard hand grasped his shoulder while another covered his mouth.

Todd jerked in shock and his heart began racing. His eyes widened in surprise as he watched two soldiers materialize out of the vast nothingness.

One of the two soldiers nodded to the unseen man behind Todd. The hands came away from his mouth and shoulder, and as he continued to stare at the craggy, thin-faced man before him, he slowly realized it was Joe.

Joe had changed dramatically in a short time. Todd looked at a face lined with permanent fatigue and a body as lean as a snake. His eyes were hooded as he looked at Todd and his slight smile was devoid of any of its former warmth.

He frightened Todd, just a bit. The Joe that Todd had known back in the days before everything went to crap had always had a relaxed, soothing air about him.

Not anymore.

The man standing in front of Todd was as taut as the cables holding the Golden Gate Bridge. When he had been a police officer, Joe had worked out, but still had some extra padding from the hazards of police sitting. This man was all muscle, hold the fat.

"Thought you were dead," Joe told Todd.

"Thanks. I thought you were, too," he replied.

As they walked back the way Todd had come, another soldier materialized from the side of the trail. Todd realized he had passed the soldier without ever seeing him. These silent men were spooky.

Within ten minutes, they came upon a well-camouflaged jeep and, after a mostly silent forty-five minute journey, they parked in front of a big rock.

When the driver punched a handheld keypad, the rock moved and the jeep rolled into a narrow alley under the mountain. Todd thought he had seen it all, but this was something entirely new.

"What is this place?" he asked Joe.

"It's a shadow base, military made," Joe answered. "With all the stuff you know, you didn't know about these?"

Todd looked at Joe and saw a glimmer of a smile. This new Joe was closed and hard to read, so Todd was not sure how to answer him.

"I didn't know about this. How many are there?"

Joe cut his eyes to the side to look at Todd as he said, "Who knows?"

Todd had the feeling that Joe did.

After the jeep was parked in this underground garage, everyone got out and walked toward a side door. As the group walked through the nondescript door, Todd's eyes widened for the second time that day as he uttered, "What the fu..."

Todd lost the power of speech mid-sentence.

A complete, underground military base opened up before him. In the middle of the base sat a Black Hawk. The mountain's carved-out belly housed an entire small military town.

Looking up, Todd noticed the dome. He had wondered how they had been able to get it in. Now, he knew.

"Let's go," Mister Hard Hands growled at him after he paused to look up.

Ahead of him, Joe turned, stopped, and waited for Todd to catch up.

"Don't give him any reason to bite you," Joe told Todd.

When Todd looked at him in alarm, the ghost of his old friend Joe smiled back.

Todd followed Joe as he walked into one of the nondescript buildings. Inside, Todd stood in awe as he stared at the most advanced computer systems he had only seen in his dreams.

Joe watched Todd's expression turn from one of anxious fear to something close to love. He had noticed the uneasiness Todd had tried not to show; he did not blame him. If he had been a stranger in the company of the men of Congo Force, he would have been uneasy, too.

"You're drooling, man," Joe told Todd with a slight grin.

"I wish I could make love to this room," Todd replied with a dreamy expression in his eyes.

"Just don't leave anything sticky," Joe said with a slight laugh.

As Todd sat down at one of the stations, Joe outlined what he needed him to find. Joe had not been able to narrow down where Beanie might be to less than three-hundred and seventy-two areas in the country. He did not have the time or the resources to go to each one.

Before Todd got started, Joe asked him the question that had been burning in his mind from the moment he heard from Todd.

"How did you find out Beanie was still alive?"

Todd stopped gawking at the computers and turned to Joe. "There was a blog about rehabilitation in people who had been declared dead. I was coasting through it – 'cause I'm morbid, you know – and someone started writing about this chick from a small town who had died and then been resuscitated.

"Anyway, I would have skipped right over it, but the blogger started detailing her physical description, what she had done before her accident, then about the accident itself, her husband, what he did, and, the coup de grace, the town they were living in at the time of the accident.

"It was you and Beanie, man. They were talking about the husband disappearing. That was you. They were talking about the woman being in the hospital, not getting any better, dying, being brought back and then going through the dead rehab."

Todd stopped for breath. "I sent you that message as soon as I finished reading the blog, but that's the last time I saw anything about Beanie."

It had been something short of a miracle that Todd had contacted him right before Joe was about to kill the Presatical and possibly be killed himself. It was equally a miracle that Todd had contacted him again and at such a short distance away from Congo Force.

The whole Todd situation was a bit unsettling, but Joe believed it was simply his own paranoia acting up.

Joe sat down beside Todd and heard what had brought

his old computer friend so far from home.

"It was bizarre after the Chaos started, man. People didn't know what to do or what was going on. Most of your cop buddies joined the New Military. "They caught me jacking passes from the Feds a month before the world went to shit." Todd gave Joe a crooked smile. "I didn't stay in for long once the govs saw I could jack into anything."

Todd frowned and continued. "You know who turned me in? That fucking dweeb Tony from the game room." Todd paused and said in a quiet voice, "I made sure he went to the front during the first attack."

Joe was not the only one who had changed. There was iciness to this new Todd, a coldness that was more than the typical anti-socialism he had had before.

"Oh, mama, I am in love," Todd said as he happily tapped away on the keyboard. "Beam me up, snotty, there's a new play-uh in town. Hey, Joe, I'll take one of these for ho, man."

Well, maybe Todd had not changed that much.

"They're not mine to trade, man," Joe told him. "You can take whatever you want, as far as I'm concerned – after you find what I need you to find. Then, we'll take you to a safe point and you can go wherever."

"Dude, I'm going with you. Those crazy asses I was hanging with didn't know jack about anything but collecting guns. Half the guys couldn't even shoot straight.

"Crazy is a mild term for those jokers. They shoot each other on accident and laugh about it," Todd said as he shook his head.

"Todd, it's not my decision. It's gotta be group. These guys don't know you. I'll vouch for you, but my word only goes so far."

Joe shook his head. "They've . . . we've all been through a lot in the past week."

Todd did not reply. He had already sunk into his familiar, comfortable cyber world. While he waited for his hacked databases to load, he turned to Joe and shrugged, as if to say, whatever happens happens.

Joe patted Todd's shoulder as he left. Before he got to the door, Todd called him back.

"She's in Baine, Minnesota. She was moved from some dipshit town in Illinois to another dipshit town in Minnesota a few months ago," Todd said. "No matter what else they can hide, nobody can hide the tax breaks they get," he continued as he exited the Internal Revenue's website.

It took Todd a moment to realize Joe had not answered. When he turned around, his heart started racing as he looked into the wickedly dark and dangerous barrel of a gun in the hands of a madman.

16.

Baine, Minnesota. When Joe heard those words, something snapped inside of him. The tensions from the past year coupled with the tornado of his own life made Joe lose it when he heard those words.

One of the most covert operations in the military was the disposal of bodies that had endured the military's "gentle" persuasive techniques used during interrogations. If relatives or friends came looking for their missing loved one, the standard answer was that they had been relocated in a witness protection program sponsored by the military.

The military had no such thing.

On the inside, when some unfortunate guest met his end during a "session," his remains were cremated and dumped in the garbage. Long ago, someone had coined the phrase "going to Baine, Minnesota" to signify a body that was about to disappear completely.

The pall those words had cast when Todd told Joe that Beanie was in Baine, Minnesota, was almost unbearable. Just as reflexive as a cat under attack, Joe had whipped out his gun and pointed it at Todd's head. Insanely, he had wanted to pull the trigger on his friend.

In between two breaths, Joe found himself again. His mind cleared and he lowered his gun. Todd was visibly shaken and Joe could see the sweat pouring down his face.

"Sorry," he simply said.

"I don't know what's got into you, but I didn't have anything to do with anything. You hear me?" Todd said with a quiver in his voice.

"I know, man. Baine, Minnesota, isn't real. It's military code for getting rid of bodies," Joe said as he tucked the .32 away. "Sorry. It just hit me when you said that."

Joe sat down beside Todd. Todd scooted a few feet away from Joe. Joe smiled at Todd's uneasiness.

"My crazy isn't catching," Joe said

"Yeah, well, just the same, I'm gonna stay over here,"

Todd replied.

Joe and Todd sat quietly, each deep in his own thoughts. "Why would the IRS have Baine in its system, then?" Todd mused out loud. He turned back to the computer. "Hang on a minute," he said as he rapidly typed on the keyboard.

"That's the only time it's mentioned in all the IRS databases. Strange. One time and that's it. With something like that, you'd expect to see it somewhere else; anywhere else, for that matter."

Typing some more on the keyboard, Joe tried to follow, but Todd was a speed demon on the Internet. He had five windows up and was rapidly flipping from one to the other as he looked for information.

"I'm stumped. Every reference to Baine, Minnesota, comes up empty." Todd sat his chin cupped in his hand. "Unless we're looking at logistics. War Freak uses a five-point code for a cross-section latitude/longitude."

Todd took out a key ring holding a number of flash drives. He plugged one of the drives into the USB port on the front of the computer and loaded his contraband One-Sega program.

"This is a little doozy I was working on for the gunners. It locates munitions dumps by a six-point code the military uses."

Todd typed something on the keyboard and the programming language appeared on the screen. To Joe, it was beyond Greek – it looked more like something out of an alien movie.

"Look right here," Todd said as he pointed to a set of letter and numbers. "I just need to tweak this and it'll give me a five-point code to break that acronym."

More alien language. Joe watched Todd type and click, but he did not comprehend a thing the computer wizard was doing.

"I am a cyber god," Todd said smugly. The old Todd was coming back.

"Look here: this is the longitude, this is the latitude, and this is the x-factor coordinate," he said as he plotted the numbers on a virtual map. "Once you get the numbers down, you straight line them, kinda like connecting the dots.

"Next, you x the points and find the crossover where they all connect. It's really just a take on star navigation, except you don't use a sextant. Once the points connect, that's where you find the treasure."

Joe tried not to show his impatience. He did not need to understand how Todd did things, he just wanted the results. However, after pulling a gun on his friend moments earlier, Joe was not really in any position to make waves with Todd. He needed him.

"So, connect your dots, already," Joe said lightly.

Todd looked uneasily at Joe. He was hoping to God that Joe was not going to go ballistic again. Todd had burned his bridges with the gun gang, and Joe and his group were his only resort. Todd did not, could not, go it alone in the new militaristic world.

"Garth, Arkansas. That seems to be where the dots connect," Todd told Joe quietly.

"Then, it's Garth, Arkansas. What the hell is in Garth, Arkansas?" Joe wondered aloud as he stood up. "How big's the town and what's close by?"

"Military isn't close; town's only got around sixteen hundred," Todd read from the city data information he had pulled up on the computer. "Other than a big-ass mountain, there's nothing to speak of."

"I don't know where we're going after Garth, but I want you to come with us," Joe told Todd as he was leaving. "I can't guarantee anything, not even your safety. We're on dangerous ground and it's not gonna let up any time soon."

Todd simply nodded at Joe as he left. He was relieved that he would be with the soldiers, but, at the same time, he felt a premonition of extreme danger ahead. He could not tell if it was just his nerves or a real sense of bad things to come.

Todd shook himself to clear his head. He downloaded the information they needed onto a flash drive before he, too, left the room.

As the men bunked down, lights inside dimmed to

simulate night. Outside the base, the real night cast its dark shadow over the mountain. A lone dog, sniffing its way to its next meal was the only thing moving. He was, however, not alone.

Positioned behind brush only twenty feet from the entrance to the base, a single figure in battle fatigues kept silent watch on the surrounding area. Even though Joe had intended to sleep, the round and round whirling of his mind prevented him from his much-needed rest.

He relieved Jackson and hunkered down with the night. As he watched the landscape, shadow dancers appeared from out of the hard ground. Joe knew it was a trick of his mind, a hallucination, and a bad one at that since these illusions normally happened during the heat of the day.

Nevertheless, he watched the phantom warriors as they wove in and out under the moonlight in a rhythmic battle dance. A part of him knew it was all in his head as he followed the ghostly spears jabbing at enemy wraiths.

A part of him did not care. If this was a sign from some higher entity, it was not needed. Joe was prepared to battle and die at any time; he had been since the chaos had begun in his own life. His only care was Beanie. He had to live long enough to find and protect her.

This time, nothing would take her away from him. Not even death. Joe felt he could battle the Grim Reaper for Beanie. He felt he could win.

The night wore on. As dawn approached, the shadow dancers faded back into the ground. Joe cautiously moved toward the entrance of the base. Once inside, he heard the bustle of his men as they prepared to leave. The briefing he had given them the night before had been brief.

While he had not lied to his men, he had not told them the whole truth. They knew Joe's presumed dead wife was possibly in Garth, Arkansas, under the care of the military. What he did not tell them was that it was not the military, but the Muveed who were watching over Beanie.

He did not want to delve into his dealings with the Muveed. Not yet. He needed to see for himself what they were now up against. Joe was strongly inclined to believe the Chaos had fundamentally changed that sinister organization, just as it had changed every other organization and country in the world. There was no reason the Muveed would be exempt.

Loading their supplies, the group boarded the Blackhawk and set the dome to open. Todd was a little queasy as he sat down, but there was nothing he could do. He could not very well walk to Arkansas.

Well, he could, but he sure did not want to. As he sat, one of the men offered him a protein bar. This was the first sign of goodwill any of the soldiers, besides Joe, had given Todd since he had joined them.

The dome opened and the helicopter took off.

The bright sky belied the deadliness of the world. This was one of the strongest signs that Nature truly did ignore man. No matter what was happening, no matter who was fighting whom, Mother Earth kept on going.

Flying as the crows, it did not take more than five hours for Congo Force, plus one, to arrive on the east side of Garth, Arkansas. As the helicopter flew over Garth, Joe and Abba looked down and commented on how it looked like any other small hick town.

The mountains made landing anywhere but east of Garth difficult. Although, there were level strips of land alongside the vast hills, the abundance of thick pines made landing impossible except for an area a few miles to the east of the small town.

Their landing created little stir in the area. A few cows lifted their heads as the Black Hawk landed. As the men disembarked, the herd looked curiously at them and then went back to the business of eating.

Joe took off his flak jacket and unloaded most of his weaponry. He did not want to go in like the combat soldier he was and end up scaring Beanie. That was the last thing he would want to happen.

"Abba, Jackson, with me," he said, motioning to the men. "Heff – you and the rest, stay here. If we lose contact and we're not back in one hour – take off."

Heff nodded. Elk started taking off his flak vest and joined Joe.

"I'm coming with you," Elk told Joe. "You need me for backup. These two," he said as he motioned to Abba and Jackson with a grin, "ain't much for looking behind."

Joe was not going to argue with the big man. He had initially planned for just the three of them to go in for reconnaissance, but having Elk with them might come in handy.

As the foursome was leaving, Loco tossed Joe a sheathed knife. "Never know when you might need a good blade."

Joe caught the knife and slipped it into his belt. Although he had his own blade, Joe had accepted Loco's treasured knife and understood the significance behind the gesture. Loco had faith that he would be back.

The group cautiously walked toward the coordinates Todd had given them. As they drew closer, Joe led them through the heavily wooded area with extra care. He remembered what Liz had told him about the Muveed defenses surrounding the town of Normal. He did not want himself or his men to become victims of those deadly perimeters.

The appearance of the small, gated subdivision was exactly as Liz had described a typical Muveed community. A heavy gate and a double guard house, one on each side of the road, were at the entrance. As Joe and his group eased closer, they noticed the spiked brick fence set at an almost forty-five degrees surrounding the homes inside the gate. The fence was purposely impossible to climb without shredding oneself. Although one could try to throw a hook over and scamper above the spikes, Joe had not doubt there were nasty surprises waiting on the other side.

Coming from the southeast, the first indication that all was not right was the wide open gate and the lack of guards in the guardhouses. The front area looked unkempt and as they approached the gate, a lone dog slinked out.

On the main road, Joe noticed how deserted the small subdivision appeared. Grass was growing unheeded, and trash was blowing around the homes and up and down the street.

As they walked the street, they checked each house they came to. Most were deserted, their occupants fled or taken. In one home, the men came upon a man on a respirator. Although the electricity had apparently gone out long before, solar generators were keeping some of the power on.

The man on the respirator never responded to the men. Standing around the comatose man, Joe and the others were at a loss as to what they should do. They did not have the equipment to care for this man. Yet, they did not want to be so heartless as to leave him to his eventual fate, whether it was at the hands of cruel men or roaming, hungry animals.

In the end, there was only one thing to do and Abba gently did it.

Walking to the next house and the next house, they came upon more of the same. Helpless people had been left with no caretakers and the cruelty of the situation tore at each of the group. Each took a turn helping the helpless.

In one of the last houses on the street they came to had a man with one leg who immediately woke when they entered his room. Abba jumped and Jackson let out a little yelp that he quickly camouflaged as a sneeze.

"Who are you?" the one-legged man demanded.

"Congo Force, Twentieth Division, Sector Four," Joe answered automatically.

"Get the fuck out of my house," the belligerent man barked.

"You tell us what went down and we'll leave," Joe replied as Elk stepped into the room and glared at the man on the bed.

The one-legged man made a quick decision to cooperate. As he briefly related what had happened to the town, Joe felt his earlier conjuncture that Muveed had fallen apart was true.

Apparently, according to the man, when the Chaos started, more and more of the caretakers were being called away to other places. He himself was a former engineer at one of the Muveed outposts and lost a leg that year in an explosion set by a former Muveed and her accomplice.

As the man continued to talk, Joe realized he was talking about Normal. Pumping him for more information on Normal, the man told Joe very little he did not already know. The main answer Joe was looking for was where Vincent had gone, but the man knew nothing about the head of the insidious organization.

In the enclave of Muveed in Garth, the one-legged man continued, all of the Muveed caretakers, guards, and other personnel had eventually left. It quickly became every man for himself and those who could not leave were left to rot.

"Is there a woman with red hair here?" Joe asked.

The man shook his head. "There's only a few women; none of 'em have red hair. There's one down at the very end that's still here; she brings me stuff from her garden. There's another one across the way, but all she does is sit on her back step all the time – if she's still here."

Joe nodded as he and Elk left the room and joined the others. This was one they could take with them; his value was his knowledge of engineering and of Muveed. If his handicap proved to be too much of a hindrance, Joe would have no problem putting this member of Muveed down in an instant.

"Jackson, you come with me and you two stay here. If this guy wants to go with us, I think we should take him. Whatever he knows about engineering could help and if not, we can always ditch him.

"Scout around here and see if he has anything worth taking, specifically, tools and manuals," Joe said as he and Jackson walked out the door.

His heart was racing and his palms were sweating. He wanted to find Beanie and he was scared to find her. It had been so long and so much had changed in him that he did not know if she would even want to be with him.

In the house across from the one they had just left, no one was inside. However, just like the one-legged man had told them, they found the female occupant on the back step.

At least, what was left of her. Animals had made off with bits and pieces, and what was left was putrefying. From what he could make of the body, the woman had been very large. It was not Beanie.

Stepping away, Joe looked down across the open backyards. Most were bare, but one was alive with plants and miniature gardens. He and Jackson moved toward that particular house and he knew this was where he would find her.

Before they could enter the backyard, a bulky man came around the side of the house, aiming a small semi-automatic at the pair. The man handled the gun like a familiar friend. He was one soldier who would not be easily overcome.

The man silently motioned the pair to the ground as he circled behind them. So quickly that he had no time to react, the man knocked Jackson out and immediately pointed the gun at Joe. As Joe was beginning to kneel on the ground, he saw the soldier unsheathe a wicked knife. Joe had no illusions about what might happen next.

Before he had a chance to use it, thought, Joe rolled on his back and barrel-kicked the man to the ground. Grabbing the wicked knife, Joe turned the blade on the hefty man. He covered the man's mouth to prevent any dying sounds to escape since Joe had no idea how many other hostiles might be around.

Lifting Jackson to his feet as his fellow soldier tried to clear his head, Joe looked again toward the backyard gardens. Even though Beanie liked gardens, she had never produced one as bountiful as this one. He cautiously walked toward the garden. When he turned to look at the patio, he stopped dead in his tracks in shock.

As he stared at a piece of pottery holding a lineus vine, his breath caught and his blood turned to ice. The clay plant holder was newly handcrafted; the glaze was so fresh it looked wet. He recognized its signature swooping style. He had watched as similar items were made on a spinning pottery wheel. For years, he had been part of the process –

hauling the wheel, mixing the clay.

Only one person had made pottery items like this. Only one person in the entire world had perfected the swooping downward lip on the top edge and the swooping upward lip on the bottom.

He felt he was losing his mind as he stared at the pottery. Only one person could have made it and that person was dead.

Joe turned with a face drained of blood as the back door opened. The apparition stepped toward him. With dry mouth, he could barely croak out a word that, once again, turned his world upside down.

"Mother."

17.

The wraith drifted to Joe. Holding a hand to her throat, she looked quizzically at him with no recognition in her eyes. Joe looked back as if seeing a ghost.

He had seen her dead in the hospital room. He had been with her when she had taken that last breath as she lost her fight with the cancer eating away at her throat. He had seen the monitor flat-line and had been rushed out as nurses tried to revive her one last time.

In accordance with her wishes, she was to be buried straight away. No open-casket, no viewing, no mourners; his mother had wanted her life celebrated instead of waked.

This was the person Todd had tracked down. Joe instantly realized that Todd had no way of knowing that his wife and his mother ironically shared the same name.

A gamut of emotions ran through Joe. Aside from shock, he was in stunned happiness to find his mother, Mary Abigail Daniels, was alive. At the same time, he was devastated that Beanie was still out there, somewhere.

His mother did not recognize him. She had a puzzled expression on her face as she looked at him. When she looked beyond him with a smile, the hairs stood up on the back of his neck. His sense of danger immediately flipped on as he turned to face the person at which his mother was smiling.

Two stone-faced men in running shoes and track clothes were standing at ease on the side of the garden. The taller man was standing directly behind Jackson and Joe could tell by Jackson's expression that he was not free to move. As Joe leaned to get a better look, he saw the gun pressing into the small of Jackson's back, out of view of Joe's mother. When Joe looked up, the shorter man shook his head slightly, as if to say, do not upset the woman.

"You need to leave," he told Joe quietly. Shorty stepped closer to Joe as he spotted the dead man on the side of the house. His eyes hardened more and he pointed his already drawn gun at Joe.

The four were locked in a macabre pose when a loud shattering startled them all. As they looked toward the sound, the woman on the patio gestured sternly toward them with a pointed finger.

"Miss Mary, we're okay here. Why don't you go back inside and we'll be right in," Shorty said.

Joe's mother took the cane she had propped against the back steps and carefully walked toward the group. Shorty continued to plead with her to go inside.

This was the woman Joe remembered. She never backed down and she never did what anyone told her to do if she did not want to. Her independence and freedom had been the most precious aspects of her life. She had instilled Joe with the same ideals.

As she approached the group, the puzzled expression in her eyes began to clear. Shorty quietly spoke to Joe and told him that he would skin him alive if he hurts or upsets the woman.

Shorty watched Joe like a hawk as Miss Mary ran her hand over Joe's hair and lightly slapped the back of his neck. He is transfixed as he sees the tears drip from Joe's eyes as Joe and the woman Shorty has been charged to protect embrace.

When his mother slapped his neck, Joe broke down. It was the way she had always greeted him; it was her familiar loving gesture. This was the mother he knew. But, did she know him?

Taking his hand, Abigail Daniels led Joe into the house. The others could do nothing but follow. Warily and in great confusion, Jackson let the tall man pat him down before they entered the house.

Shorty looked at Joe closely. Without a change in expression, he said, "Miss Mary, is this Joe?"

Mary nodded as she continued to hold one of Joe's hands between the two of hers. Joe regained some of his composure and noticed that his mother was remarkably calm for someone who had just found her son after so many years.

As if reading his mind, Shorty told Joe that Mary was on heavy sedatives for the chronic severe pain from the experimental operation that had taken nearly all of her throat, but saved her life. Time had lost meaning for her, and her conception of days, months, and years passing was nil. Today, tomorrow, and yesterday all blended together in her mind. To her, every day was a day in the present.

Mary released Joe's hand and signaled to the tall man that she was ready to rest. Out of Mary's sight, Shorty continued to hold the gun on Joe and Jackson. When she left the room, he brought the gun to the tabletop. He did not aim it at either of them.

"What's going on?" Jackson asked Joe.

"That was my mother. I saw her die in the hospital," Joe said in a bewildered tone. "I don't understand. I thought my wife was here, not my mother."

Joe looked at Shorty, and Shorty shook his head as he told Joe, "All I know about her back history is what I just told you, and that's what my bosses told me.

"She's been antsy lately, talking about, I guess, you. She kept waking up and writing to us she was dreaming of a man with dark hair named Joe."

"I don't know what I'm supposed to do," Joe said, as the enormity of finding his mother hit him. "She doesn't know who I am, does she?"

"I ain't a doctor, but I do know the meds she's got to take mess with her mind. At some level, she knows you're connected to her, else she wouldn't have touched you like she did."

Shorty looked up as Tall Man walked back into the room. "And she sure wouldn't have invited you inside."

Shorty looked more relaxed as he talked. "The man you killed out there was a lackey for Muveed. I recognized him from the barracks in Iowa. He's the second one to come here in the last week."

"Mac and me buried that first one in the woods. They were both part of cleaner crews." Tall Man paused. "Good riddance."

Joe looked at both of the men. "You're not Muveed?" he asked.

"Used to be, before the Chaos," Shorty replied.

"Why didn't you leave with the rest?"

"Couldn't leave Miss Mary, and this place was as safe as any out there, as long as you stay away from the red zones."

"Red zones?" Jackson asked.

"Northeastern coast was invaded last week about the same time as that Argentina assault was going on. Maine, Nova Scotia, parts of New York, parts of Pennsylvania, New Hampshire and Massachusetts fell in hours."

"What about that guy up the street? Why didn't you help him and the others?" Jackson asked. The boy was suddenly full of questions.

Mac looked at Jackson and said, "He won't let anyone but Miss Mary come close to him. The last time I tried to get him to come out, he threw a full bedpan at me.

"The others weren't in our care. Our main priority is Miss Mary."

Joe pulled out his radio and Tall Man, real name Eric, pulled out his gun. Mac motioned him to put it back.

"Are there any military close by that you've seen?" Joe asked Mac.

"Nothing close. But I can't guarantee there aren't more Muveed slimes coming around. They know this place is here."

Joe sent Jackson to bring Elk and the one-legged man to the house, and then he radioed Loco to load up and fly to the middle of the community. While they were waiting, Joe told Mac and Eric a very brief synopsis of what had happened in the past few days and why he thought his wife was in the Muveed settlement. Neither looked surprised.

Joe realized they had seen and heard much more than his own story. They were Muveed, after all. Since they had gone beyond loyalty to his mother, he felt he owed them a loyalty, of sorts.

When Loco landed, Joe and the others met them outside. While they were disembarking, Joe and Jackson filled them in on what had happened and who had been in the house. Todd looked strickened when he learned Beanie was not there.

Joe put his arm around Todd and thanked him for everything he had done to reunite Joe with his loved ones. It just happened to be a loved one from his distant past, Joe told him, but finding his mother alive after all these years was beyond priceless.

"I'll keep looking, Joe. I won't stop 'til we find her, I swear."

"I know, man," Joe told Todd. "I have faith in you."

At that, Todd looked a little relieved, but he was still on edge. Joe's behavior the night before had stayed with him, and when he learned Beanie was still missing, he had been afraid Joe would take it out on him. Again.

The men of Congo Force were speechless with amazement and still had open mouths when the shots rang out from the woods.

The radio in Abba's hand exploded as a bullet hit it and pieces flew everywhere. Abba dropped, unhurt, to the ground instantly. As the men hit the ground, Mac and Eric ran from the house and took up positions on either side of the SUVs in the driveway. As all opened fire, they could hear the screams from the woods.

Crouching close to the ground, Heff and Rock raced to the edge of the woods just in time to see a group of civilians with guns running. As they gave chase, they cut them down, one by one.

Heff and Rock returned to a rushed evacuation. There had never been shots fired between Mac and Eric and the townspeople, but there had been words. It had gotten so bad that when they needed supplies, Mac and Eric took to raiding unoccupied homes instead of going into town.

That was where they had been when Joe and Jackson had encountered them. Their backpacks were loaded with food and assorted items taken from an abandoned farmhouse two miles away. Although they cringed at leaving Miss Mary by herself for any length of time, circumstances had forced them to find food or starve.

They always traveled together when raiding. One to stand guard and watch, and the other to gather supplies. The country had become a dog eat dog nation, with every man looking out for himself.

As Mac and Eric quickly packed light bags for their charge, Joe watched his mother and sympathized with her confusion. With her hands, she was protesting that she did not want to leave her home. Joe tried to comfort her by telling her they were taking her to a new home.

A new home. Joe had a good idea where to take her, but they would have to find a military base to refuel before they could go. The best place for his mother and her keepers would be the place where he and Liz had hidden away.

Joe shuddered slightly when he thought about what he would find when he went back to the hunahas kanitis. He hoped no one had found the survivalists' camp. It was so well hidden within the massive rock formation that finding it was almost impossible.

It was the "almost" part that worried him.

He felt he was putting his mother in a different danger, but it was safer than where she was at present. Unless things had changed within the past few months, it would have an ample supply of food, water, and fuel.

Everyone loaded onto the Black Hawk. Joe briefed Loco on the location of the North Dakota camp and Loco took off. The airspace they had to cross was not without danger, but most of the danger came from the locals who had gotten their inexperienced hands on weapons of war.

While they were in the air, Joe explained to the rest about the camp and about Liz. Mac and Eric did not seem to recognize Liz from Joe's description. He had half expected them to, since they were Muveed.

He told everyone about Liz. He told them how she had made him leave when she started to die. He related how the Muveed had killed her with a remotely activated poison. Mac and Eric nodded knowingly at this.

Instead of heading straight into the hills of North

Dakota, the crew, plus four, touched down at another shadow base outside of Graceville, Nebraska. This shadow base was almost an exact replica of the one in New Mexico, right down to the paint on the buildings. What the military lacked in imagination, it made up for in, well, nothing.

As they touched down, Joe unlocked the door and Jackson ran in to release the dome. The Black Hawk soe in the air again, touched down inside, and everyone disembarked.

Mac and Eric looked around cautiously. They had not been fully accepted by the group, but they both knew it was only a matter of time. Both of the men had been glad to be rid of their Muveed membership and needed some other cause to fight for. They needed to belong to the side that would make a difference.

Miss Mary was given quarters in the women's section of the base. Although it was close quarters, Mac and Eric would not leave her side. The oaths they had sworn to Muveed paled in comparison to the serious responsibility they had accepted when they became the old lady's caretakers. There was nothing and nobody they would not battle to defend her.

Joe valued their protection of his mother. More than anything, he needed to know she would be taken care of and her keepers would continue to protect her with their lives. He needed to know they would be her surrogate sons when he was gone.

18.

There was no movement on the ground for miles. The landscape looked bleak and lifeless. Passing over the nearest town of Fort Berthold, they noticed the signs of a vicious battle. A large area to the east of the town had been obliterated and a crater the size of a small lake had burnt the earth.

A good majority of the homes and businesses in the town had been damaged. Flying low, Joe could see the wanton random destruction and surmised that civilians had, once again, gotten their hands on weapons they had no business touching.

The town was uninhabited. As the chopper passed over the town as they headed west, no residents came out to see what was circling overhead. The dust and debris covering the streets and vehicles looked undisturbed.

When they approached the survivalists' camp in the northwestern corner of North Dakota, the remote area looked even more remote from the air.

Touching down close to the huge rock encompassing the camp, Joe felt a little shaky. When he left the survivalists' camp so many months before, he had left a dying Liz. Now, he would have to face that.

He remembered exactly where the hidden entrance had been. He told the crew that he and Elk would go in to make sure everything was safe. He did not have to tell them he was going in to bury his friend. They knew he needed to do this alone.

The crew watched as Joe and Elk walked away. From the vantage point of the helicopter, it appeared as though Joe and Elk disappeared into the rock formation. The hunahas kanitas illusion was perfect.

Everything looked exactly as Joe had left it. The first place he went into was the cabin in which he and Liz had stayed. It was the last place he had seen Liz alive.

As he walked in the door, he prepared himself for the

sight and smell of a decaying body. Liz would have been long dead by now. He needed to find and bury her body before bringing his mother into the camp.

There was no body in the living area. Motioning Elk to stay where he was in the doorway, Joe searched the rest of the cabin with no luck. He looked in cupboards, closets, under bunks – nothing.

There were only a few possibilities: Liz had either recovered enough to leave or she had been discovered. The second explanation worried Joe.

Joe and Elk walked outside. The camp was not that large. It would take the two of them less than fifteen minutes to do a walk-through.

"I'll go this way," Joe said as he pointed to the east. "You catch that way and we'll meet in the middle."

Elk nodded and started walking the west side of the perimeter. Joe started the other way. As he came around the side of the cabin, he spied the papier-mâché rock that Liz had hidden their truck under when they had first arrived. It was so lightweight it had drifted all the way around the cabin, blown in the wind like a giant beach ball.

He nudged the fake rock with his foot and it moved easily, belying its heavy look. As it rolled a few feet, Joe caught a glimpse of something shimmering under the light film of dust that covered the entire camp.

A gold ring glinted in the sunlight. As Joe brushed the dust and debris away, he saw the ring a bit more clearly. Liz always wore the ring. It had been her mother's and Liz's father, Sergeant Matters, had given it to her on her sixteenth birthday.

The ring was plain gold with a tiny diamond set in the band. It was of no great value except to the girl who had lost her mother much too early in her life. Liz had told Joe that throughout everything in her life, she had never taken off the ring.

That was still true.

As he cleared more dust, he saw the ravaged body. The dry air had preserved the corpse, and although the leathery skin had taken on a dark hue, he instantly recognized Liz as he knelt on bended knee beside his friend.

He did not know why she had crawled outside to die. Either her mind had gone by that time or she had purposely died in the open under the sky. Whatever the case, she was now free. She was now with her family.

Joe looked up as Elk came around the corner. Dropping to one knee, Elk patted Joe's shoulder in sympathy. Without a word, Elk got up and walked toward the shed behind the cabin.

Returning after a minute, Elk looked around and found a spot close to the edge of the camp, next to the rock formation. As he started digging, Joe silently thanked his big friend for picking the right place for Liz. It was out of the main living area, but close enough that she would not be forgotten.

After they placed the body in the grave, Joe took the shovel from Elk and thanked him. He wanted to be the one to cover Liz one last time.

"Please get the others now," Joe told Elk.

Elk walked to the entrance. Even with Joe leading the way earlier, Elk still could not see how they were able to go through solid rock. Pulling a box of lemon drops out of his pack-kit, Elk pulled a Hansel and Gretel and left a trail of candy to help lead him back inside the camp.

The others joined him at the entrance. Out of earshot of Joe's mother and the one-legged man, he briefed the soldiers, including Mac and Eric, on the body they had found and buried.

Inside the camp, the others looked around the survivalists' lair. The illusion of walking through rock was still in their minds as they walked around the small camp.

The group found Joe finishing the sad task of burying his friend. They gathered round and listened as Joe talked about Liz.

"Liz saved my life. She didn't know me, but she risked her life for me. She didn't have to help me. She could have walked away. She made a choice, but it cost her her life."

After the burial, Joe and the others split apart to search the cabins for supplies. Gathering all of the extra food and fuel, Joe directed the group to deposit it in the cabin that he and Liz had stayed in.

Joe did not want his mother staying in that cabin. It was not because he considered it a shrine; it was because he felt queasy about putting his newly living mother in a house where death had so recently visited.

"Joe, we need to do something about the chopper," Loco said, breaking Joe out of his reverie.

"Take this," Joe told him as he pointed to the papier-mâché rock. "You can break it up and put it around the chopper."

Pointing to some netting that had been left on the ground by the previous inhabitants, he said, "That should do well enough for the top."

Mac walked up to Joe as he was talking to Loco and Abba about camouflaging the helicopter. Although he was still reeling slightly from all of the activity within the past twenty-four hours, Mac was the type of man who could take it all in stride. He was Muveed, after all, as his family had always been. Yes, he was Muveed. Or rather, he used to be.

He had no idea if the organization was still in the United States. They had lost all contact with Muveed four weeks before. Most of the other Muveed in the community had deserted and left their charges to their own fates. Mac and Eric were the only ones to remain and the only other Muveeds who had come to the community after it fell apart had been cold-hearted cleaners.

What he had not told Joe was he knew more about his mother's condition than he had led Joe to believe. He had not told Joe that he and Eric had been there when Miss Mary had been resuscitated under the orders of Vincent. He had not told Joe that both he and Eric were field surgeons and had assisted in the experimental surgery on Joe's mother.

Vincent wanted to keep the woman alive for some unknown reason. Mac did not know why and he was not foolish enough to ask. He was also not foolish enough to tell

Joe that he and Eric had been part of the team in charge of making sure the patient stayed comatose until orders from Vincent dictated otherwise.

That had been the only time in Mac's long career with Muveed that he had deliberately disobeyed a direct order. On the infrequent visits by Muveed superiors, either Eric or Mac would give Miss Mary an injection that simulated a comatose state.

No one outside the community was the wiser. Others inside the settlement either did not care or empathized with the situation. The Muveed caretakers knew that their charges were alive at the whim of Vincent.

All of these thoughts ran through Mac's head as he waited for Joe to finish giving directions. When Loco and Abba left, Mac had Joe's attention.

"How long will we be here?" Mac asked.

"I don't know. There's some things that we need to get done and it could take anywhere from a week to a few months. We'll make sure you're stocked."

For Mac, the answer was as much as he had expected.

"Thank you, man, for taking care of her," Joe continued. "I don't think 'thank you' is near enough for what you guys are doing for my mother. The best I can do to repay you is make sure you're safe until we get back."

"Can the entrance be sealed?" Mac asked.

"Yeah. I'll show you when we leave. If you're gonna seal the entrance, when we come back, we'll drop a sign with a fly-over.

"You've got enough rations to last a few years, fuel for the generators for at least eighteen months."

Joe shook his head slightly. "We shouldn't be gone nearly that long, but ... just in case. Look, there's an old jeep behind the last cabin that was still running the last time I was here. If we're not back in, I don't know, a few months, well, use your own judgment."

As Joe and Mac walked back toward the others, Mac realized he had officially and ultimately severed his lifelong ties to Muveed.

The one-legged man, Stewart by name, was making himself at home already. He had hooked up the DVD player he had insisted on bringing and was playing one of the movies he had brought. His box was stuffed to the brim with retro movies and TV shows.

Abba was in the room talking with Stewart. When Joe looked at them, Abba shook his head. The group had taken Stewart because it seemed he would be useful to them, but Joe realized he would be more of a liability than an asset.

All in all, they had done a good thing by bringing Stewart with them. Joe knew Abba was feeling guilty about the mercy killings he had done back in the community. This one good thing was good for Abba. He needed it.

Supplies were unloaded, stocked, and Congo Force walked the camp with a check-through before everyone settled down for the night. The plan was to stay only one night.

Joe spent the evening with his mother. While talking to her and reading what she wrote on her constant notepad, he saw that she had retained bits and pieces of memories. She talked about her life before she came to America, but it was simple recollections of sensations she experienced as a very young girl.

She knew Joe and she seemed to know that he was someone close to her. However, she did not acknowledge him as her son. Joe felt a melancholy wistfulness for the mother he once knew.

Even so, as she stroked his hair and thumped the back of his neck, he knew that fragments of his mother were still there. He hoped with proper care, more of the mother he remembered would also remember herself.

When he asked Mac about her condition, the former Muveed had very little information. Joe surmised that Mac knew more than he was telling him. Because he had risked his life to care for his mother, Joe was willing to let it slide. For now.

Joe had seen her die. She had flat-lined and Joe had been rushed out of the room. The doctors worked to revive her, but it was useless. She was gone.

Well, not anymore. Here she was, alive and kicking. If his mother could come back from the dead, there was enormous hope that somewhere out there, Beanie was alive and waiting for him.

The night passed quietly and morning came quickly. Before they left, Joe hugged his mother tight – he did not know if it was the last time he would see her. Joe showed Mac how to block the entrance and after he finished, Mac handed him a sheath of papers.

"It's got every location of Muveed towns and settlements that I knew of," Mac said. "I wrote down all the security codes, the passkey codes, and door lock codes. There's a list of every person that I knew at each facility. I don't know if it's gonna help you, but it can't hurt."

Once again, this man from Muveed surprised Joe. Joe shook his hand, looked at his mother as she waved good-bye, and then he left.

Abba was the last one out. As he was stepping through the hunahas kanitas, Mac stepped up behind him. Mac slipped him a key and whispered something in his ear. Abba looked back sharply at Mac and put the key inside his flak jacket.

The chopper took off. Joe looked back at the rock formation that had become a safe haven for one of the two women in his life that he loved beyond himself. As the distance grew greater and greater, Joe felt his eyes tearing up. His future was uncertain and he did not know if he would see his mother again.

As they flew across North Dakota, Joe turned his mind to something that was concerning him: Todd. He had been unusually quiet over the past two days and Joe was worried he was headed toward a breakdown. He could not have that happen at this stage in the game.

Joe quietly asked Heff to find out what he could about Todd's present state of mind. He watched as Heff took the seat next to Todd. Whatever Heff found out would affect whether Todd stayed with them as a working member of the team or as a dependent.

Joe hated to be brutal, but chaotic times called for hard decisions. Unfortunately, as the de facto leader, Joe was the one who had to make them. He was responsible for every man on the team and he could not have one man jeopardize everyone else. Joe hoped Todd never became a liability.

Moving up front, Joe consulted with Loco on their fuel supply. Outside of Upper Red Lake in Minnesota, Joe remembered a shadow base where they could stop and refuel. He gave Loco the coordinates, from memory, and then settled back to catch a few.

The motion of the helicopter lulled Joe to sleep. In a half-awake, half-asleep state, he dreamed of Beanie trapped in a box, screaming for Joe to let her out. In his sleeping mind he was digging and digging into soft earth that was collapsing around him as fast as he scooped it out.

Beanie's cries became fainter and fainter, and were replaced with a heavy sense of despair. In his dream, Joe felt impending death and saw the hand holding a knife dripping with blood. A man with his face covered sat in a chair and held out his hands as the disembodied hand holding the knife approached.

In his dream, the scene shifted. The knife holder began slicing his own hands until they were covered in bloody gloves. A mirror reflected the knife holder, and as he lifted the face he had smeared with blood, Joe awoke with a start.

The fresh dream stayed with him. He knew his face was the image in the mirror. The blood on his hands would send him straight to hell.

Joe looked around. Each man on his team was deep within his own self. They all had ghosts and demons to face, but none more so than Joe. He was leading these men into something deadly and he could not give them the choice to turn him down.

He was embarking on a selfish mission and he needed Congo Force with him. The formation of an idea, a martyrdom, had been growing in his mind. He had finally come to terms with what he was and it empowered him and terrified him.

It was time to end it all. If it meant sacrificing himself and the men in his troop, then so be it. The alternative was damnation and doom.

He did not need answers, for he knew most of them. What he needed were questions and he needed to be the one with the power to ask them.

19.

Death was all around them. The scattered reports and garbled radio messages they had heard over the past few days since leaving North Dakota had been full of retreats, defeats, and death.

The brilliant military moves that had been applauded by the populace only weeks before were now backfiring. The military might of the New Americas was shrinking. What had once been the strongest force in the world was now on even par with other disorganized countries. Worldwide bedlam threatened to destroy what was left of society.

Anarchy was the rule of the day as individuals chose to join with the enemy or defend their own turf against their neighbors. Old grudges and ancient feuds surfaced, and many men, women, and children paid a bloody price.

The center dissolves, Joe thought as he and Elk walked around a deserted tourist's camp near Murphy Lake, Indiana. Days before, they had landed at the shadow base outside of Upper Red Lake for Loco to refuel. Joe's intent had been to touch down at the main United States New Military base in Nova Scotia. From there, it was a hop-skip from Greenland to Iceland, until they were able to land in the United Kingdom.

Those plans went to shit when they crossed over the Illinois line into Indiana. Touching down in a clear spot alongside Murphy Lake, the group disembarked. Loco and Heff were making some minor repairs to the rotary and the rest were cleaning their guns or otherwise occupied.

They heard gunfire and hurried into position as a full compartment of battle-hardened soldiers from 46th Company emerged from the eastern woods. Joe recognized the soldier in charge. The man with the big gun had been the police officer who had taken Joe for drinks after Joe had saved that couple from thugs in Meader, Nebraska.

"Man, never thought I'd see you again," Officer Wayne, now Sergeant Wayne said as he quickly pumped Joe's hand.

False World

"Can't stick around and talk; we've got mooks on our tail. Whole east coast is gone. Not the same ones from South America; that one got wiped out by the French Alliance. Don't really know who these mooks are, but they've got some heavy shit they're popping us with."

"How far did they push?" Joe asked.

Sergeant Wayne looked back over his shoulder and pointed to a forest of trees about four hundred yards away.

"See that line of trees?" he said. "About a mile back from there."

Joe whipped around. "Load up!" he yelled at his men. Turning back to Wayne, he offered to load up his group.

"Yeah, thanks man," Wayne said as they ran toward the chopper. "There's a munitions dump five miles from here; we gotta restock ammo. After that, we'll hoof it – got a place we're trying to get to near the Lakes. It's army-fortified and they won't be able to find it."

"Shadow base?" Joe asked as they climbed aboard the Black Hawk.

Wayne looked surprised as he sat down. "Yeah. You know about it?"

Joe nodded as he reached inside his jacket for the list of shadow bases.

"Here's a list of every shadow base we know of," he said as he handed the paper to Wayne.

Sergeant Wayne took the paper and looked at it. He looked at Joe and asked, "How'd you get this?"

"Doesn't matter. It's for real, if that's what you're worried about," Joe replied. "Do you know if any of the West Coast has been hit?"

"Just a few isolated spots, but nothing compared to the East Coast – it's almost completely gone. Only a little over half the people got out before the attacks started. Man, it was a coordinated attack. There must have been thousands of ships lined up and down the coastline. All at once, they attacked with some kind of modified nukes."

Wayne paused to catch his breath. "Nothing's left. New York City's pretty much wiped out. DC's gone, but since the government moved to Texas, that didn't matter much. What I don't get is why they had to bomb the shit out of Savannah. Savannah, man, of all things."

Joe smiled at Wayne's incredulity. Joe understood his disbelief. But, then, when did war ever make sense?

"Somebody's responsible for what's happened. Whoever started this whole damn thing could have stopped it. Now, it's up to us and before it's over, the whole world's gonna be wiped out." Wayne shook his head. "If I could find the son of a bitch, I'd gut him and let him die in the dirt."

Joe bid Wayne and his men good-bye and god speed as they touched down at the munitions dump. They had not wanted to join with Joe; rather, Wayne told him, they were going to stay and fight to defend their homeland. Joe admired his loyalty and patriotism.

He did not have the heart to tell him it was all for naught. The country Wayne believed still existed had imploded in on itself and the only things left were anarchistic groups trying to rule their own roosts.

Change of plans. Joe told the Congo Force troop their only option to enter Europe would be through Northeastern Russia – Siberia, to be exact. The problem would be a matter of refueling once they left Alaska, but Loco assured Joe he knew of a refuel point halfway across the Bering Strait.

Three days later, Congo Force landed in Anchorage, Alaska. Anchorage was eerie. The landscape was devoid of human life, but the city teemed with people. Invaders had not touched the entire state even though it was closest to the Russian border.

It seemed to have been an overlooked opportunity. However, unbeknownst to Joe, Russian and Chinese forces had previously planned an invasion of the Americas, starting with Alaska.

Time was not on Russia and China's sides. The rapidly shifting alliances in the chaos of the world stopped all plans of an Alaskan invasion. Russia, China, and other Eastern European countries switched from ally to enemy in such rapid succession that collaborators one day were usually deadly foes the next.

Anchorage, and the rest of Alaska, had been spared – temporarily. Changes in the world did not guarantee the safety of any nation, except maybe Australia. The country down under was still watching with folded arms as the rest of the world spiraled down the toilet. Other nations had thought to try to conquer the Australian continent; they always thought twice when they came up against the heavily fortified coastline.

Alaska had no such security. Their coast was not lined with underwater mines like Australia. Instead, their security was their remoteness from the lower forty-eight states. To mount an attack on the continental United States would require advancing over two thousand miles through rugged Alaskan and Canadian territories.

In Anchorage, the troop replenished their dwindling supplies and refueled. The remaining military at Fort Benn in Anchorage were more than happy to help their fellow soldiers.

Abba secured maps and locations of current safe zones within the European continent. The only problem with the safe zones was that they were subject to change at any time.

Landing in Nome, Congo Force refueled one last time on friendly soil before heading west toward Russian. As there were no more fueling posts, Joe hoped Loco was right about the refuel station midway across the Bering Strait.

The wind began picking up when they left the coast. Joe watched as Todd's face turned a few shades of green before he vomited in a barf-bag. Elk, Jackson, and Heff were starting to look a bit peaked, which was unusual for the seasoned travelers. The constant buffeting from the strong wind was affecting half of the crew.

Forty minutes after leaving the Alaskan coast, the helicopter passed over a small inhabited island in the middle of the ocean. They flew past it and touched down instead on a second rock and ice covered island. Joe remembered this island from countless maps he had seen over the years.

Big Diomede was the Russian counterpart to the United

States' Little Diomede Island. Since the eighties, Big Diomede had been uninhabited. With the changes in the world, Joe had known they would be taking a chance when Loco told him about the island and its hidden fuel sources.

"We're landing on the east point side of Big Bay crevice before we go to the fuel dump," Loco told Joe as they touched down. "Just in case they've got somebody at the old Soviet base and we have to persuade 'em to give us some gas," Loco said with a wink.

Joe knew exactly what he meant. He was prepared to terminate with lethal force anyone who crossed the wrong side of his path. He had become hardened to the death he dealt out. Way back in his military days, long before the chaos, each death he was responsible for had haunted him. He would have nightmares of someone's mother accusing him of murder as she wiped her son's blood on Joe.

Not anymore. His dreams these days were of the people taken away from him. He could have cared less for anyone else, save those close to him. He would not give a tear if he had to kill a stranger. The compassion in his heart had long since dried to sawdust.

It was some Russian stranger's lucky day. The island was totally and completely deserted, save for a few seals on the rocky beach. Even though they were Russian seals, the men of Congo Force decided to invoke amnesty as long as the seals swore allegiance to . . . well, hell, no one could think what country to swear to anymore.

The light-hearted mood continued as the men started to invent names of new countries. The United States of Abba, the Coalition of Cool, and the Rock of Futile and Shifty Alliances were a few of the names the crew bounced around.

Loco was right on the money. The fuel dump was well hidden, but not well enough. Loco found it within thirty minutes of landing. The temperature in the fuel reservoir was stable, so they did not have to worry about the flow. The only problem they encountered were the curious, newly sworn-in seals that kept getting in the way.

The crew bunked down for the rest of the day in the

deserted Soviet base. Joe looked at the men around him and was grateful that they were willing to go with him on a mission that could only end in sorrow.

He had not given them the complete story, only bits and pieces. He had been afraid they would not believe him. The only person in the troop who knew most of the story was Todd. Before they crossed over into the land of ten thousand nights, he owed the total truth to Abba, Jackson, Elk, Heff, Rock, and Loco.

His conscience had gotten the better of him. He needed to tell the men who would be risking their lives for him the reason they were risking their lives. He could no longer be selfish and if they decided to turn around and head back to whatever home they could find, he would go with them without a fuss.

Much to Joe's surprise, the crew seemed to believe what he told them about the Presatical, Muveed, and the alliance of bastards who truly ruled the world. A few months before they would have been incredulous and skeptical; with the craziness and absurdity in the world since the Chaos, anything that made the least bit of sense was something they wanted to grab onto.

At the core of each man was the very simple belief they could bring the anarchy and disorder present in the world back into stability. They did not expect to be able to make worldwide peace; that had never been an option throughout history. Instead, they wanted to bring the balance back.

Joe was slightly amazed that the men understood even the things he did not speak aloud. Several times, he caught one or a few nodding in comprehension, as if an idea or thought finally made sense.

It was hope. Plain, everyday, sometimes misplaced, hope. That was what he had given his men, that and a sense of purpose.

They felt a chance to right a wrong and a chance to set things straight. They were resigned to possibly never seeing stateside again, but it made little difference. If they did not attempt to intercede in the affairs of the world, the country they remembered from months back, the New United States of the Americas, would quickly become like the poor countries their military had bombed into submission.

Breaking open a bottle of bourbon Jackson had found when he was looking for the typical Russian vodka, Heff poured shots all around. Raising glasses, the men saluted each other.

Congo Force took off that evening. All of the troop, except for Todd, had some military experience on Russian soil. The biggest concern would be fuel for the helicopter, but even that was minor. They would be able to commandeer what they needed from Russian bases or airports.

The last news Abba had picked up the day before had been good for Congo Force. Russian troops had been decimated and the remaining soldiers were in the southern portion close to the new Chinese border. China had forced its way into Russian territory to the west and north, and Russia was at the point of just trying to hold on to what they had left.

Landing outside of Pueten, Chukotskiy, Congo Force saw the devastation of war had touched the Russian village. Most of the town had been leveled in a blast and only a few remaining structures teetered on their foundations. There was no sign of life.

They restocked with whatever they could find, but the pickings were very slim. Whatever villagers escaped the bombardments that destroyed their village had apparently taken everything. Aside from a few cans of beer and a sack of hard candy, there was nothing of value left in the village.

Joe and his men climbed back into the helicopter. After consulting with Loco and looking at several East European maps, Joe formulated a route which would avoid any armed conflict. He was prepared, however, for his troop to cut down anyone who stood in their way.

They all knew the score now. Harsh conditions, bad or no food, and a good chance they would not live to see the New Year were all part of what they had committed to when they agreed to accompany Joe across the European continent.

It was not that different from the military they had recently left. The job was the same, but now they had complete autonomy. Although they were all willing to listen to Joe's lead, each of the men knew that he himself could veto or change their course.

Refueling was not going to be a problem. Sitting beside Loco, Joe noted more than two dozen abandoned air bases as they flew over the forbidding Russian terrain. Four hours into their flight from Pueten, they touched down at one of the deserted bases.

Even though it looked deserted, Congo Force was on alert. They had been in situations that looked peachy on the outside, but turned rotten very quickly. This situation proved to be one of those.

From out of nowhere, shots rang out. Congo Force hit the ground and took up positions behind whatever they could find. Motioning Jackson and Rock to move around behind the enemy, Joe and the remaining soldiers barraged the area to the north with an overload of firepower. Jackson and Rock unloaded in the same direction as they quickly moved into position.

The fight was over almost as quickly as it had begun. The silence was deafening. Jackson and Rock looked at the dead soldiers, nine in all, and not one of them looked to be over fifteen years of age.

"Ohhh, shit," Joe heard Abba moan. Turning around, he saw the blood saturating Abba's t-shirt and dripping off his fingers as it ran down his right arm. Joe grabbed Abba and dragged him into the chopper.

Ripping the t-shirt, Joe saw that the bullet had passed through Abba's shoulder. Opening the med-kit, Joe took the morphine pen out and jabbed it into Abba's leg. Abba immediately passed out and Heff grabbed a cauterizing gun to seal the entrance and exit wounds.

Loco refueled as fast as he could and the troop took off. There was no way to avoid the ambushes they might run into, Joe thought as he helped dress Abba's wounds. It was dumb luck the second base they had touched down in Russia had little boys playing soldiers.

Abba was still passed out as they moved and secured him on a bench seat toward the back of the chopper. Todd looked visibly shaken, either from the attack and his participation or from Abba being shot. At that moment, Joe did not have time to deal with him.

After stabilizing Abba, Joe returned to the front of the helicopter and sat beside Loco. The earth below him had been devastated by dirty bombs; the land would take thousands of years to recover. As he watched the cold, dead land moving beneath them, he wondered what other surprises this foreign land had in store for them.

He hated it. He hated the bitter, depressing land. He hated the dirty poverty they could see even from high in the sky. He hated that he was so far from the country he used to call home. He hated that he still did not have his Beanie.

Heff made his way to the front and squatted down between Joe and Loco.

"I've been thinking. Have you seen any airplanes, MIGs, choppers, anything that could fly?"

Joe shook his head. It was puzzling that they had not encountered any other aircraft to challenge them. The situation was uncharacteristic of the extreme measures the Russians had always taken to secure their territory.

He had not thought beyond getting into Europe. If they had met with any military challenges in the air, they would have been sitting ducks. A helicopter versus aircraft designed to destroy was a no-brainer.

It did not make sense, but what did nowadays?

"Here," Joe said to Heff as he rose from the chair. "Ride shotgun for awhile."

After checking on Abba, Joe crashed on an empty bench. The motion of the helicopter soon lulled him to sleep. For the first time in a long time, Joe slept without dreams.

20.

Loco had a newfound respect for the Black Hawk helicopter. Flying across thousands of miles in weather ranging from tropical to frigid, the Black Hawk more than proved itself.

Built for war, the helicopter was equipped to survive more hardships than a normal helicopter. Loco had tested this theory over and over again during the past few weeks. He was thankfully surprised the old bird was still flying through it all.

Amazingly, Loco had not had any problems refueling as they headed west across the vast Russian territory. The few skirmishes Congo Force had been involved in had ended quickly and decisively. Amateur gunmen, mostly young boys, were always overwhelmed by the massive firepower Congo unleashed.

Abba had been the only one to suffer any injury. Joe had blamed himself for Abba's injury. Since then, Joe had only let a few men off the copter during each fuel stop. Everyone was going stir crazy by the third day in Russia.

Everyone was itching to leave the cramped helicopter except for Todd. Todd was dealing with different problems. As each day passed, he became more and more despondent. He felt out of his element; he was not a soldier, but he had chosen to join Joe's group out of desperation and fear.

He was much more at home in front of a computer screen playing at soldier in online competitions. The first time another person's blood splashed onto him, his depression dropped to a new low.

Joe had been keeping an eye on Todd and the rest of the men. He knew they were tired of flying with only short breaks when Joe felt it was safe enough to land. Joe was tired of it, too. He knew it was only a matter of time before he had a mutiny of sorts on his hands.

They had flown thousands of miles across Russian land. As much as he could, Loco was keeping them along the northern border, as it was a less likely place for whatever home-based military Russia had left.

Last stop before they crossed into Finland was depressing. Flying over Kangas in the Republic of Karelia, the crew witnessed what they had been seeing since they began crossing the Russian territory.

Kangas looked like so many of the villages and towns they had seen: deserted, desolate, and death. As they continued westward, they began seeing more and more emaciated corpses scattered in village streets. Worse than countries at war, there was no help for the helpless when an entire world was at war.

It tugged at Joe's soul. So many innocents had suffered because of the actions of the Presatical. The long line of control he and his predecessors kept over the leaders of powerful nations had finally ruined the entire planet.

Joe could picture in his mind how the control had been destined to unravel. As more and more nations became autocratic, control was more valuable than gold. The despots who came into power would want no part of the Presatical's iron fist.

The balance had been breaking even before the keys to the Book of the Deceived had been lost in the fire. The loss of the savant's knowledge merely tipped the scale for the downward spiral of chaos that ultimately caused the world to fall to pieces.

Throughout his travels over the last year, Joe had seen the results of absolute control. He had also seen the results of the absence of control. As much as he hated to admit it, the Presatical had been the check-and-balance that had kept the worst of the despotic tide at bay.

But, he had also been responsible for the abject misery in Joe's own small corner of the world. The Presatical or Muveed or some other organization similar had been at the heart of the collapse of all things that held meaning for Joe.

Someone would have to pay. Joe had not lost his hate; he had buried it deep where no one could see, for to see the black feeling Joe carried inside of him would be as if looking into hell itself.

These horrible feelings of hate surfaced as the helicopter passed over fields of ice and snow. Memories of his time with Beanie at the Ice Hotel in Jukkasjärvi, Switzerland, triggered the repressed, but not forgotten, need for vengeance.

The hardened men of combat sitting beside Joe subconsciously drew away from him. Although Joe gave no outer signs of his anger, those sitting close sensed the seething menace inside of him and his terrible lust for blood and murder.

Life would never be the same and he could foretell how it would end. Although he had gained back his mother, he was no closer to finding his wife than he had been when he had first started looking for her. After having his hopes rise up and down, he could not admit, would not admit, she might be dead.

After he had taken care of the tyrants who needed to die, he would be done with it all. It would be time to rest the deep, black rotting sleep of the dead. He would run no more.

He had no fear of dying. He only wanted to make sure those who truly deserved death were rewarded with a proper sendoff to the hell he would throw them into before he joined the fray.

The dark ice reflected Joe's mood. The occasional fires he saw burning below them made him think of the fires of Hades. Not a religious man, Joe nonetheless believed that when he died he would be reunited with those who loved him.

His mother would be well cared for. Max and Eric had taken care of her for so long, she was more their mother than she was Joe's and they were more her sons than he was. Joe's reunion with his mother had come far too late. It was just as well since he predicted he would never see his mother again.

As the helicopter touched down outside of Helsinki, Joe was so deep in thought he did not notice the lights burning at the airfield. As they had crossed the northern part of Russia, they had all noticed the lack of electricity, but had quickly deduced it was from the overall lack of everything.

Guns drawn, Joe and Elk stepped out of the helicopter just as a full squad of soldiers erupted from behind the sole building on the airfield and squared off with them. The odds were not in favor of Congo Force.

A smallish man stepped out of the defensive formation the squad had established. He laid down his weapon and approached Joe with his hand out and Joe could see the fear on his face.

"You have no fight," the man told Joe as he approached closer. "Guns, but no fire them," he continued in broken English as he motioned toward his comrades. "Please, you come to the inside where warm."

Distrustful, Joe shook his head and said, "We'll stay with the helicopter. We just need fuel."

"Ah, fuel plenty. Tell your man is behind white building"

Joe saw that the man was shaking; he did not know if it was from fear, cold, or something else. As he continued to try to persuade Joe to come inside the lone building, Joe noticed with each entreaty, the man moved closer and closer to Joe and away from the rest of his men.

Joe kept his gun leveled, but otherwise, he did nothing to deter the man's approach. Within ten feet of Joe, the man stopped and Joe could see the terror in his eyes. Something was not right.

The man was mouthing something, but the light snow that had just started swirling around them was obscuring his face. Joe had a bad feeling about what the man was trying to say without words.

As he approached even closer, Joe raised and steadied his gun. Joe grabbed the terror-stricken man by his collar, and dropped him behind Elk.

When the first shots rang out, Elk and Joe dropped to the ground. There was no cover and they were sitting ducks in green camouflage contrasting sharply against the white snow.

Jumping from the open doorway, Rock, Jackson, and Heff hit the ground shooting. Decimating the other side was not easy until Abba grabbed the portable anti-armor rocket launcher and let loose on the snow-covered enemy from the doorway of the helicopter.

Dangerous as it was, Abba knew they had no other choice. Eventually, the thirty or so men would overcome Joe's seven-man crew.

The increasing snowfall and the semi-enclosed belly of the Black Hawk muffled the report from the blast. Loco was thrown to the floor of the cabin, striking his head against the instrument panel on the way down. Joe and Elk felt the wings of super-heated air as the missile Abba launched passed over their heads.

What was left of the other side scattered. Joe, Elk, and the scared little man rapidly climbed aboard the Black Hawk. Joe did a quick head count and ordered Loco to take off.

Loco had pulled himself up off the floor by the time the others jumped onboard. Flying in the snowstorm would be hazardous, but staying on the ground with an unknown number of armed enemies would be courting a certain death.

A small stream of blood was dripping into Loco's left eye as he took off. His abrupt lift threw everyone off balance. Todd grabbed Jackson's hand as he slid toward the open bay door. The soldier was much heavier than he looked and Todd felt like his arm was about to be pulled out of its socket.

"Get in here, you stupid shit-eating asshole!" Todd bellowed at Jackson, who was hanging half out of the helicopter. More than the words, the tone in Todd's voice shocked Jackson into action and with a sudden burst of energy, he regained his footing and climbed back into the chopper as it started to level off.

What had happened was so totally out of character for the computer guru that everyone stopped what they were doing and just stared. Joe tried hard to fight the image in his mind of Todd turning into Sergeant Matters, but he could not. Todd had roared like Sarge had done so many times during Joe's stint in the old military.

It was neither the time nor the place, but Joe could not stop the roar of laughter. As soon as Joe broke the laughter ice, it spread to all the others. Even Todd, though red in the face from embarrassment, joined in.

The little man Joe had rescued (or abducted – Joe was not sure which he should claim), did not get the joke. He looked at the man's puzzled expression and laughed even harder.

Joe surmised the man might not understand that in times of extreme stress and danger, the best way to get back on focus was to laugh. Deep belly, thigh slapping laughter was the number one way to relive tension.

As soon as Joe gained a bit of control over his somewhat out-of-control laughter, he went up front to help Loco navigate. The pilot had blood all over the left side of his face, but he was alert and somewhat pissed.

"Next time one of your boys decides to shoot his wad off in my helicopter, tell him to give us a warning before he jerks off," Loco angrily told Joe.

Joe started laughing again, but quickly turned the laugh into a cough after Loco shot him a killer look.

"Okay, man, I'll make sure they know. Hope it doesn't happen again," Joe said with a smile.

"Okay," Loco replied with a nod. "Shit. This mother hurts like a bear trap," he said as he touched the knot forming above his left eye.

"There's a commercial airport across the Gulf in Estonia – should be enough fuel there unless it's been raided. Just keep going due south toward Tallinn, maybe twenty, twenty-five miles."

Joe remembered the small airport in the southern part of Tallinn. Years and years ago, when he had been part of Sergeant Matters' team of soldiers, the squad spent a month at a base near Tallinn, Estonia. Joe and a few others had explored the outskirts of the city and had stumbled upon a small airport.

Joe remembered the fuel storage tanks were awkwardly located close to a major highway. It was unlikely the tanks had been moved from that area, but he wished they could find a less public area to refuel.

Looking at the water as they crossed the Gulf of Finland, Joe noticed nothing. No boats, no skaters on the frozen sections of the Gulf – nothing. In the distance, Joe could just barely see the outline of the shore of Estonia and the closer they came to land, the more of nothing Joe saw.

From the air, Tallinn looked like it had been hit by a nuclear blast. Parts of the city were smoking and other parts were buried in an ice-covered shroud. As they flew south, Joe and the others watching from the air could detect no movement.

The airport had been annihilated. Parts of planes and other aircraft were scattered up and down the short runway. One of the fuel tanks was burning and Joe was worried about the close proximity of the other.

Landing a distance away from the burning fuel tank, Jackson, Elk, and Heff took off on reconnaissance before the others tried for the fuel. They returned fifteen minutes later.

"Didn't see anything, Joe," Heff said. "Whole place is deserted."

"Loco, it's me and you," Joe said as he ordered the rest of the men off the chopper. If it blew, it would only take him and Loco out. Joe was really hoping it would not blow.

Before he and Loco went to refuel, he took Abba aside and told him to keep a close eye on the little man from the base in Finland. Something about the little man made Joe uncomfortable.

The tanks were only forty yards apart. A shift in the wind and the fiery fuel could travel to the stable tank. Unfortunately, they did not have a choice but to try. The Black Hawk was almost empty and Joe did not think they could make it on foot in the harsh winter conditions of the North Territories.

Loco and Joe flew up and circled the airport before touching down close to the tank. They quickly began refueling and both were on a crazy edge waiting for the heat they felt from the tank burning nearby to set fire to the stable tank. Joe did not want to transform into a human torch, but the increasing heat was making him feel like he was not too far from flaming on.

As soon as they finished, Loco put to the air and touched down next to the rest of Congo Force. After the men had climbed aboard, they took off to the south.

Joe calculated one more fuel stop before they reached the remote village of the Presatical. It was not a miracle they had made it this far; something was pulling Joe back to the land of the despot of the world.

Joe sat next to the little man. "Who are you?" he asked.

"I have business in Helsinki. When I go to airport two days ago, men in soldier clothes, they take me prisoner."

The little man's eyes started tearing up as he continued. "I not rich; the men keep me and then you show up. They make me stand out front for you to shoot first."

A perfectly plausible explanation, but something was off-kilter about the little man and Joe could not put his finger on it. All he knew was that he had a sense of discomfort around the little man.

Joe trusted his senses. He probed more into the man's life and actions over the past few days, but nothing he said yielded a clue to explain why Joe felt he could not trust him.

The little man kept thanking Joe for saving his life. He told Joe he had heard his former captors as they made plans to chop a hole above the frozen water of a nearby pond and drop the little man into the icy lake – alive.

It was not the first time in history that a man had been used as a human shield. All through time, men had been more a commodity than individuals with rights and freedoms of choice.

The scenario was very familiar to Joe. This was how the power nations ruled. It was how they viewed the people they should have been protecting, but exploited on the battlefield instead.

Still, there was something disconcerting about the little

man that made Joe uneasy. He had never seen the man before, yet, along with the uneasy feeling, there was a hint of recognition. He just could not figure out what he recognized in the man.

    Joe never, ever forgot a face. Joe never, ever forgot treachery. He had a long list of payback and it was fast approaching time for Joe to settle the scores.

21.

At an airbase outside of Brezno, Slovakia, Congo Force almost exchanged friendly fire with a diminished squad of American soldiers. Like countless other squads based in Europe, Africa, and Asia, the small American military unit stationed in Algeria had been trapped in Europe when the Chaos erupted.

The abrupt termination of all military communications made the men expendable. Like lost sheep, the men had been trying to find their way back home. Saudi coalition forces had been on the march toward the base the American soldiers had been stationed at in Bechar, Algeria.

Major Bill Whilton had been monitoring communications of the approaching enemy. When he heard Nigerian and Moroccan forces join in with the Saudis, he mobilized his small unit and got the hell out of Bechar.

Their journey was fatal to half of the unit as they tried to cross the Mediterranean. They commandeered a ramshackle boat from a reluctant fisherman in a little village on the northernmost Moroccan shore.

The crossing should have been quick. There was only twelve miles of open water to Tarifa, Spain. It should have been an easy crossing.

Within two miles of the Spanish shore, a family in a speedboat attacked them. Because the soldiers were not expecting to be facing death at the hands of a father, mother, and three children, they were taken by surprise when the shots starting ringing out from five semi-automatics.

Seven of Major Whilton's men died within the first twenty seconds of the attack. The element of surprise did not last – the remaining men in the unit opened deadly fire and killed all five. The nightmare of shooting children would stay with them for the rest of their lives.

After that devastation, the major and his men began hiding during the day and moving only at night. Stealing cars as they could and walking when they had to, it took them several weeks to reach the Slovakian border.

During their trek, they saw firsthand the inhumanity of man against his fellow man. Entire towns were crushed and burned. Bullets did not discriminate; unknown enemies killed men, women, and children of all ages.

War was war, but what had happened in the towns and villages Major Whilton and his men passed through was genocide of the human race. If what they saw in Europe reflected what was happening worldwide, then the population of the world must be declining at a rapid pace.

Man was destroying man, deliberately and without thought to the consequences. Extinction was a very real threat and it deeply disturbed Major Whilton. A theology student before he enlisted in the new military, the major believed in an afterlife.

He also believed he was living in the apocalypse.

There was no way to avoid the devastation. One of his men, a young soldier with a tender heart, ate the bullet of his own gun after seeing one too many of the innocent dead. The others understood why he took his own life. But for a hardening of their own hearts, they would have joined him.

When the squad arrived at the base outside of Brezno, they saw a United States military helicopter. Some of the men believed it to be a mirage. Two men in the squad dropped their guns and ran toward the first friendly sight they had seen in a long, long time.

Joe saw the men running toward him and was drawing his weapon to take them out. As he squeezed the trigger on his semi-automatic, Jackson's hand came out of nowhere and shoved the gun down.

The spray of bullets landed in the snow ten feet in front of the running men, making them stop in their tracks and drop to their knees with their hands clasped behind their heads.

"They're some of ours," Jackson told Joe quietly. Joe shook his head to clear his mind and realized he had been on defensive autopilot for too long.

Stupid people running toward men with guns had a little

to do with it, too. If not for Jackson's quick action, Joe would have cut the two men in half.

After everything was sorted out and no one was in imminent danger of being shot, Joe and Major Whilton drew off to the side to talk.

Joe filled the major in on the situation in the United States at the time Congo Force had left. The major told Joe of the dizzying array of coalitions in Western Europe. The allies one country might have on any given day could, and did, change overnight.

"I don't know how you'll make it across Russia," Joe told Major Whilton. "We barely made it, and we had the chopper."

"What choice do we have?" the major replied. "There's nothing here for us and we'd rather be on home territory than where we've been. It's a death sentence staying here."

The major gave Joe a questioning look. "Why are you here?" he asked.

"Unfinished business that needs to be finished," Joe replied coldly. "You're welcome to come with us, but it's my command if you do."

Joe could not know that with those words, he changed the course of Major Whilton's life. The major had been thrust into a position of leadership and he had excelled, but he was tired of making all the decisions, good and bad. He had been waiting for someone to take over and, secretly, this was the driving reason for his return to the States.

The major was ready to turn his eyes away from the world and toward the heavens. When he told Joe he had been a theology student before the collapse of society, Joe grinned.

"If you want to lead some prayers, go for it," Joe said. "But, you won't lead anything else if you join Congo," he continued with a hard look in his eyes.

The major felt his soul sigh with relief. He was a soldier by default; his real life was as a man of the cloth. With a handshake, he shook off the military role he had been conscripted to and took up his true calling.

Major Whilton's men were equally relieved. Though they respected the major because of his rank and his dedication, they were ready for an aggressive leader who would take charge. They were ready for someone who would lead them home.

Congo Force was now twenty strong and Joe was ready to move out. He conferred with Loco on the best way to make a final approach to Avvel, which was nestled in the mountains between Austria and Switzerland. Finding a flat plateau might be a problem.

They decided the best course of action would be to land three miles east of their destination. The terrain smoothed out the closer it came to the nearby river and landing would be less of a problem.

The element of surprise would be in their favor, too, the further out they landed the big, noisy helicopter. As they flew into Austria, Joe felt his heart racing with trepidation. The last time Joe had been in the Presatical's pissing grounds, he had ended up with a cracked skull and no memory of how he got back to the States.

The closer they came to Avvel, the faster Joe's heart raced and the sicker he felt. He began questioning why the hell he was doing this again, and what did he think he could accomplish. He knew his answer – he did it because there was nothing left.

There was another reason, a very important reason: he was the one with the knowledge to stop the world's decline into hell. If the downward spiral did not stop, the earth would be populated with only ghosts.

The blame lay on that despotic group of men and their ringleader, the Presatical. No one should have such control over a world. No tyrant should be able to decide a man's fate; only a man should have that choice.

Joe wanted to restore the balance. He was going in half-blind with little knowledge of how he could fix what was broken. All he had was the conviction that he was the key that could lock the door to hell.

Before he knew it, they were ten miles from Avvel. Joe

had been so lost in thought he had not noticed when Loco had passed over Graz, nor did he notice how intently Peter, the little man he had rescued, was watching him.

After Major Whilton briefed his crew on the change in leadership, he immediately leapt into his new role as an usher in God's theater. He likened himself to a mere guide along the terrible road of life, a guide leading those who sought knowledge of a higher place than the physical world.

Abba was the first of Joe's crew to cross over. His recent brushes with death had made him rethink the paths he had taken throughout his life. He needed to know that there was more to existence than the life he was living.

Joe returned from the place in his mind that was full of terrors and heard Loco telling Rock, who was second-seating in the front, they would have to land more than three miles from Avvel. Joe stepped to the front with a scowl.

"Man, something's happened down where you were telling me we could land," Loco told Joe as he sat in the seat Rock had quickly vacated. "Look there," Loco said as he pointed to the side.

As the helicopter circled, Joe saw the upheaval in the earth along the Inne River which ran through the Otztaler Alps. Giant boulders had been tossed carelessly from the mountain range, falling into and beside the river, thereby, making it impossible to find a flat area to land.

It looked like the area had been hit with nuclear. Joe looked at the Geiger counter to his right, but it did not register higher than normal. Looking at the destruction, Joe wondered if it was manmade or from the fist of God.

"Go north, Loco," Joe told the pilot. "We'll follow the river until we find flat land. If we have to, we'll ride it until we get past the mountains."

As they flew over Avvel, Joe noticed the small town of Avvel had not escaped the world's war. His heart dropped as he looked toward the secluded chalet of the Presatical and saw that parts of it had fallen down.

Joe needed answers and those answers were inside that cursed place. If he had to, Joe would dig through the rubble with his bare hands to find them. He had not come back to the source just to turn tail and go back home. He was here to stay. He was here to find the answers. He was here for his Beanie.

Sink holes the size of pickup trucks dotted the banks of the Inne River. On their journey upriver, Abba and some of the others witnessed the ground collapsing and sinkholes forming along the river's bank. Almost simultaneously, massive disjointed boulders pushed up from the bowels of earth itself.

The phenomenon was amazing. When Loco flew out of sight of the river, the men who were watching the riverside event would yell at the pilot to get back on track. Soon, Congo's soldiers were laying bets on the time and location of the next sinkhole.

Forty-two miles upriver, Loco found a level area to land a half mile from the razed bank. Congo Force, and their guests, disembarked and prepared for the long, cold trip south.

Abba determined it would take them the rest of the day and part of the next to trek through the mountainous terrain – keeping to the river was not an option with the unpredictable sinkholes opening up.

Marching through the mountainous elevations, the temperature was bitter cold. After only an hour, most of the men could not feel their feet, their fingers, or their faces. Oddly, the only person not miserable was Peter. He walked along the rough, snowy trails like one would walk along a city sidewalk.

Coming around a bend as they neared Avvel, the mountain trail was blocked by fallen rock. As Joe and the others looked for an alternate path, Peter pointed to a path none of the soldiers had noticed.

Joe looked at Peter suspiciously. Only someone who knew his way around the area would have known about the narrow trail leading off the mountain. The endless small stones rimming the right side of the mountain trail hid it well.

Elk and Rock looked at Joe. They were thinking the same thing. Elk cocked his head and raised his gun slightly when Joe gave him a slight nod. Both Rock and Elk moved directly behind Peter as he led the group down the steep slope. The two commandoes were breathing down the little man's neck and ready to take him out at the least sign of treachery.

Shivering with cold, the men carefully picked their way down the path. Small stones littered the trail and it took every ounce of concentration to keep one's feet from slipping out and down the incline.

The narrow path led to the northern edge of Avvel. Joe did not have fond memories of the Presatical's town, but its destruction made him sad on a larger scale. So many picturesque towns had been reduced to piles of rubble since the entire world had gone to war.

The only person in view when they entered Avvel was an old man cleaning broken glass from the front of a bakery. As Congo Force approached, the old man stopped sweeping. He looked up once and dropped his head as the group passed by.

On the surface, the old man's actions could have been mistaken for those of a cowed and beaten civilian. The past two years had taught Joe that nothing was ever as it seemed. What one might see on the surface was the first layer, the public layer. Reality and truth were usually buried deep under piles of deception.

The old man had bowed his head when he saw Peter. The warning bells started ringing in Joe's mind, but he was not surprised. He had had strong suspicions that Peter was hiding who and what he was. Peter had smilingly evaded many of Joe's questions by pretending not to comprehend, but Joe believed he understood English perfectly.

As he drew closer to the chalet, Joe felt shaky. The Presatical's hidden fortress reminded him of all he had lost in the recent past. It was a hated place.

The chalet looked worse on the ground than from the air. Parts of the centuries-old stone had been reduced to dust, while other parts had collapsed into a ramshackled mess. A fire in the remaining structure had wiped out anything that might have been of use to Joe. Papers, books, everything had been reduced to ash.

The remaining locals had not touched the place. Heff found gold plates, silver candlesticks, and an assortment of other valuable items. He was not the only one – the rest of the crew found things that would have kept local families in food and shelter for years.

No one had touched a thing in the chalet; it was as if the chalet were cursed. Well, in Joe's mind it was. The population of Avvel must have felt the same way.

Poking around the debris, Jackson and Rock discovered a depression in the rubble. When they moved the rocks away, they uncovered a passageway leading down.

Painstakingly, they removed the rocks blocking the passageway, one by one. It was a team effort with everyone pitching in. Slowly, they cleared the way.

The passageway was long and winding. Joe looked down into the depths of darkness and motioned for Peter to precede the small group going down. This way, he would be able to see if his suspicions about the little man proved true.

Peter was not ignorant of Joe's distrust and knew exactly why he was being sent first. If he acted familiar with his surroundings inside the chalet, then Joe would know Peter was connected to the Presatical's group.

It did not matter now. The mission Peter had been consigned to perform was almost complete. It had not been chance that Joe had met with Peter when he did; although most of the world had lost any sense of cohesiveness, certain parts, the important parts, still operated like they always had.

Peter had found Joe by reaching out to a person close to him. The rest had been easy; tracking the renegade helicopter was simple. With the ninety-five percent decrease in air traffic across Europe, it was simply a matter of watching the approaching blips on the radar to determine who was going where.

After two missed opportunities to unite with Joe, Peter

struck gold in Helsinki when Congo Force stopped at the airbase to refuel. After a bit of deception, Peter attempted to ingratiate himself to Joe.

He knew Joe had not trusted him from the start. That was good. It was no less than what he would have expected from Joe Daniels. Everything was going according to his plan and soon, he would reveal the truths to Joe.

But, not yet. Not until he was sure that he Joe would not destroy him for what he knew. It was not yet his time to die.

22.

The winding stone staircase was slippery with slime as the group moved further down the dark passageway. When they had started out, the temperature had been as cold at the top of the staircase as it was outside.

As they moved down, the men of Congo Force noticed the temperature increasing and the quality of the air decreasing. To Joe, it started to smell like the tropical forests he had been in with the mercenaries and, most recently, with Congo Force.

The slime grew worse the further they traveled into the bowels of the earth. Twice, Todd lost his footing and would have tumbled headfirst if not for Elk. After the second time, Elk told him if he slipped a third time, he would count that as a strikeout and Todd could fall all the way down.

The darkness decreased the further they went. It was as there was a cloying patch of inky black about twenty-five steps down, but once they passed through it, the light began to glow like dusk.

The little man Peter seemed to know his way. This increased Joe's wariness and made him even more determined to find out the true background of the man.

Joe still did not know what there was about the man that was familiar. Joe's memory was just as sharp as ever, so he felt assured that he had never met Peter face to face.

Face to face. That was it. He had never met Peter face to face, but he had numerous descriptions of the man. If he had had a sketchpad, he could have drawn the man's face just from the descriptions.

Joe's blood ran cold as he watched the little man descending into the blackness of the Presatical's hell. He had not expected the second, the nefarious man in servitude to the Presatical, to deliver himself into Joe's vengeance.

Joe felt his vision cloud with red anger. Before he could stop himself, he pushed past the others until he was directly behind Peter.

Catching the little man off-guard, Joe grabbed him by the neck with his right arm and whispered hoarsely in his ear, "I know who you are. Are you ready to die?"

Joe dropped Peter down the remaining eleven steps. Amazingly, the little man survived the fall and lay on the floor, gasping for breath.

Joe dragged him to a sitting position against a wall. Squatting down in front of him, Joe pulled out his combat knife and began with the tip of the little man's right pinkie finger.

The others in Congo Force gathered around, but did nothing to stop Joe. Those in the original crew trusted Joe while distrusting the little man from the start. Whatever Joe did, the first Congo Force had his back.

Major Whilton and his men did not understand, but they were, in a way, at the mercy of Congo Force. Even though Major Whilton's men were trained in combat, their form of "gentlemen's" training was the total opposite of Congo Force's guerilla tactics.

After Peter's screams turned to whimpers, Joe started asking questions.

"Where is he?" Joe asked.

Peter caught his breath as he answered, "He's dead. His head," Peter swallowed hard and continued.

"They put it on a pike. The crows desecrated his head and they would not let me stop it."

"Show me," Joe told him.

Peter shook his head and Joe made sure the next quarter inch was bloodier. After an initial scream, Peter passed out. Joe slapped him in the face, but he could not make Peter wake up.

Joe stood up and motioned for Abba to bring the first-aid kit he kept in his pack. Digging through the kit, Joe found the smelling salts and turned back toward Peter.

The wounded man abruptly woke.

"You're lying," Joe said to him. "I can tell when someone's bullshitting me, so you better start spilling before I start spilling more of you on the floor."

Before Joe could continue his painful persuasion, Peter began to talk.

"Please, no more," he begged Joe. "I cannot tell you where he is. If I do, they will all die," he said in surprisingly good English as he began to cry.

"Who will die?" Joe asked.

"Them. The ones who know – they cannot die," he said as he tried to stand.

Joe pushed him back down. He did not care about anything else now. The moment he set foot in Avvel, his vengeance had come rushing back and his grand plans for righting the wrongs the Presatical had caused flew out the window.

"I didn't come across the world not to find the bastard. If I have to take you apart inch by inch, you're gonna tell me what you know."

Peter nodded as he struggled to stand. Holding his wounded hand, he motioned for Joe and the group to follow him as he went through a door to the right of the stone staircase. Elk grabbed him by the collar and jerked him back.

"You're not going through there first, little man," Elk told him as he motioned Rock through the open doorway.

"Clear," Rock said as continued to explore the small anteroom. "Look here," he said reached toward a small handle in a recessed section of the wall.

"Don't touch that!" Peter yelled as Rock grasped the handle. Rock jerked his hand back.

"It's a trap," Peter said as he crossed the small room. "The real handle is behind the lower brick," he explained as he bent down to reach the handle.

Rock drew closer with his gun drawn on Peter. "One move I don't like, little man, and you'll be singing in hell."

As Peter lifted the hidden handle, a door on the opposite side of the room slid open. Fresh air poured in and cleared out the dank, musty atmosphere. A natural illumination filtered through and brightened the dusky light.

As Rock pushed Peter through first, Joe heard Rock say, "What the hell?"

Walking through the archway, the first thing Joe saw was an empty chair facing him. The second thing he saw was a portrait of a familiar face that was hanging above a stone fireplace.

It was his face in the portrait.

As the entire crew came in, they all looked at the portrait and then at Joe, who kept shaking his head. The resemblance was beyond uncanny. It was eerie that a portrait of someone who looked like he could have been Joe's twin was hanging on a wall in a refurbished dungeon halfway across the world.

No one noticed the little man as he slipped through an unseen opening in the wall. Peter's mission was finished and so was his time as second to the Presatical. It was another's turn.

Joe would have to learn on his own, Peter thought as he ran down one of the dozen corridors leading away from the modified basement. He had finished his last duty as second. He had brought Joe Daniels to his destiny.

Congo Force, with Joe in the lead, went deeper into the underground living chambers. Hearing a noise, Heff whipped around with his gun ready, but quickly lowered it when he saw the protected ones.

In the largest room in the chambers, a group of savants were gathered in a circle. Some sat upright, while others had slipped out of their chairs and were slumped on the hard ground. They all looked as if they had not eaten in a week or longer.

The men quickly got to work. Two to three men went to each of the helpless and fed them whatever they had in their chow packs.

While his men were taking care of the savants, Joe looked around and tried to get his bearings.

The legends were true. These were the Presatical's idiot savants, the holders of information that held the world hostage. Or so Joe used to think.

He had had a lot of time to mull over his place in life and he had finally come to terms with the fact that he was the only person in the entire world who might, just might, be able to turn away the horrible course of things to come.

The secrets locked in his mind needed to be released and he needed to be able to clear his conscience. He was guilty of so much, and this would help to assuage his tortured soul.

He would give the savants time to rest and recover from their week of abandonment. Then, he would test the keys locked in his brain against the savants' knowledge.

Joe was scared and excited at the same time.

Looking around for the one other man who might have answers to guide him, he noticed Peter was missing.

"Where did Peter go?" he asked the entire room.

"Shit," he heard from a few of his men and he knew Peter was probably gone for good unless he chose to return on his own. Joe did not hold out much hope for that since he had cut the tip of the little man's finger off . . . twice.

No matter, Joe thought as he helped care for the savants. He would deal with whatever happened just as he dealt with everything else life shoved down his throat.

The troop took turns caring for the savants in addition to standing guard topside. One of the most compassionate caregivers was the big man, Elk. Todd later learned that Elk had a sister who had been born with Downs Syndrome and this made him more empathetic to the plight of the savants.

Joe told his group more details about his life, what he had seen and remembered, and why the keys were so important. He did not go into the minute details, but he tried to give his men an honest synopsis of his life thus far.

Todd understood completely since he had been the one who had given Joe important information about the Presatical. Todd never thought in a million years that he would be in the tyrant's chalet. Of all the things in the world that he had imagined himself doing, this was not one of them.

On the second day, Joe tried to open the minds of the savants with the keys in his head. Nothing happened, but he noticed that they were still very weak from their forced starvation.

The third day was more promising. One of the savants

began to respond, but not verbally. When Joe spoke the keys to the group, one of them looked toward Joe and began to point toward the wall.

He would not stop pointing toward the other side of the room. Major Whilton and Abba began to closely explore the wall and discovered a door handle hidden in a recessed part of the wall. When they carefully opened the handle, half of the wall rotated loudly on not so well oiled hinges.

Joe, Rock, Elk, and Major Whilton stepped through the opening. The dark passage was not filled with the soft, natural light of the chamber they had just left. The dank air had an added smell of something sharp and pungent.

As they walked through the passageway, Joe's heart began to race and he did not know why. After walking forty or so feet down the darkened underground trail, the group emerged into a room with a door on the opposite side.

There were no clever booby traps that Joe or the others could see. There were no drop shafts or blow darts. There was nothing to suggest any danger.

Joe approached the door with extreme caution, nonetheless. As he opened the door, he caught a centuries old whiff of death. Motioning his men to stay back, Joe entered the chamber alone.

Joe's mouth dropped in shock. He knew he had come full circle, at last.

He finally understood. It had never been about power. Never. The Presatical had not been the one in control. The man Joe hated more than anyone in the world was as much a prisoner to his fate as he was its warden.

Row upon row in the dim light of the chamber allowed Joe to see. Presaticals from the beginning of known time were arranged in a careful formation of the dead. The decay of their bodies ranged from putrefied remains to little more than dust.

Plaques written in all languages gave only two dates. There were no names and no testimonials on the plaques. The only writing was the date the controllers began to serve and the date that service ceased.

Some of the corpses were still dressed in the tatters of their era. Joe could count back centuries upon centuries – he was looking at men who lived during the times about which he had only read. He was looking at history.

However, one important body was missing. As Joe searched with his dying flashlight, he could not find the one dead man who might bring him a measure of peace. The current Presatical was not here. There was no freshly decomposing body of the man Joe had sworn to kill.

As he turned to leave, he noticed two plaques on a small stand to his left. One was dated with a beginning and ending that fit with the timeline of the present Presatical as Joe knew it. This was the despot's gravestone, but where was his body?

The second plaque had the start date of two days before. As Joe held it in his hand, he felt a chill run through his soul.

EPILOGUE

The end is only the beginning.

Order attracts chaos because man cannot live without conflict. Peace is only a figment of the mind – it is not real. The concept of peace is only a short interlude in the movie of life.

The man in the wheelchair knew the truth. He knew it was not as it seemed, not even to the Presatical who was led to believe he could control the world.

The power of the Book of the Deceived was only powerful to those it could destroy. The real secret, the most powerful secret, was still hidden from even those who served it.

The world was not what it seemed. Layer upon layer of deception covered the truth, and, even when the truth was bare, man could not accept that he did not have the power to control his own destiny. He could not accept that he had never had a choice.

In the worst possible way, the torch was being passed and it would be imperative for the man in the wheelchair to control the new controller. Everything must be balanced. The time of life was almost at its end and the time of true Chaos was about to begin.

Also from www.SecondWindPublishing.com by JJ Dare:

False Positive
JJ Dare

A tale of murder, war, espionage and vast conspiracy.

Joe Daniels, thought he had at last escaped his brutal past. His placid world begins to unwind when his lovely wife Beanie is involved in an inexplicable accident that leaves her changed in every way; then ghosts from his past begin to emerge.

Watch for "False Destiny," the third book in the Joe Daniels trilogy coming in 2010!

You may also enjoy these other titles available from www.secondwindpublishing.com

A Spark of Heavenly Fire
Pat Bertram

In quarantined Colorado, where undreds of thousands of people are dying from an unstoppable, bio-engineered disease, investigative reporter Greg Pullman risks everything to discover the truth: Who unleashed the deadly organism? And why?

The Runaway
George Wright

The astonishing story of an abandoned child who rose to prominence in education, military, private sector and finally in literature—all the more amazing because it's true.

Made in the USA
Charleston, SC
20 January 2012